Praise for Robert Goldsborough
SHADOW OF THE BOMB

"The author's own secret weapon is the way he stirs in just enough period detail to make you believe it really happened this way."

–Dick Adler, *Chicago Tribune*

"Featuring great characters and wonderful dialog... Goldsborough's description of Chicago has the quality of Max Allan Collins' fiction and Erik Larson's factual *The Devil in the White City*."

–August P. Aleksy, Centuries & Sleuths Bookstore, Forest Park, IL

"In 1942 most of the newspaper coverage is on the war, but Steve Malek covers the local police beat for the *Tribune*. Readers obtain a glimpse of how the war impacted Chicago and how careful everyone is not to reveal anything on weapons development. Malek is more interested in solving the homicides than in uncovering top-secret weapons that could harm his nation if revealed. His investigation is realistic and engrossing as he works his crime beat to the delight of fans of historical mysteries. Robert Goldsborough is a fantastic storyteller."

–Midwest Book Reviews on *Shadow of the Bomb*

THREE STRIKES YOU'RE DEAD

"Goldsborough, best known as the heir to Rex Stout via his half-dozen Nero Wolfe novels, creates a prewar Chicago that is at once sinister and appealing. He also weaves an engaging subplot involving Dizzy Dean and the Chicago Cubs' drive to the 1938 World Series. An enormously entertaining caper."

–Wes Lukowsky, Booklist 100th Anniversary Issue

"Robert Goldsborough, the man who so brilliantly brought Rex Stout's Nero Wolfe and Archie Goodwin back to literary life, has returned with a new detective, all his own—and that's cause for any mystery fan to rejoice! Goldsborough is a master storyteller, providing crackling dialogue and plot twists around every corner—readers are in for a real treat!"

—Max Allan Collins, author of Road to Purgatory

"You don't have to be a fan of the city of Chicago, or '30's-era gangsters, or baseball's Chicago Cubs, or suspense to enjoy *Three Strikes You're Dead* but if you are, you will love this book! *Three Strikes You're Dead* is a very well developed and written story. Mr. Goldsborough clearly knows and loves Chicago, and provides a delightful tour! Of course, even in fiction the Cubs can't win the series. Move this one higher on your to-be-read pile."

—Sandi Loper-Herzog

MURDER IN E MINOR

"Goldsborough has not only written a first-rate mystery that stands on its own merits, he has faithfully re-created the round detective and his milieu."

—Philadelphia Enquirer

"Mr. Goldsborough has all of the late writer's stylistic mannerisms down pat."

—The New York Times on Murder in E Minor

"A smashing success…"

—Chicago Sun-Times

"A half dozen other writers have attempted it, but Goldsborough's is the only one that feels authentic, the only one able to get into Rex's psyche. If I hadn't known otherwise, I might have been fooled into thinking this was the genius Stout myself."

—John McAleer, Rex Stout's official biographer
and editor of The Stout Journal

Also by Robert Goldsborough

Robert Goldsborough

A Death in Pilsen

A Snap Malek Mystery

Echelon Press, LLC

A DEATH IN PILSEN
A Snap Malek Mystery
Book Three
An Echelon Press Book

First Echelon Press paperback printing / November 2007

Echelon Press, LLC
9735 Country Meadows Lane 1-D
Laurel, MD 20723
www.echelonpress.com

ISBN 978-1-59080-531-2
Library of Congress Control Number: 2007933586

PRINTED IN THE UNITED STATES OF AMERICA

10 9 8 7 6 5 4 3 2 1

To Janet,
for reasons that would far more than fill this page

And a warm thank-you to Karen Syed, Betsy Baird, and Kat Thompson, three great ladies from Echelon Press who keep me focused and on track–not always an easy task!

Pilsen: A neighborhood on the near southwest side of Chicago. During the late 19th Century, the area was settled by Czech immigrants, those hailing from the Bohemian and Moravian provinces of what was then called the Austro-Hungarian Empire. They named this new home after Plzen, the fourth-largest city in what is now the Czech Republic.

Although other nationalities, including Germans, Poles, Slovaks, and Lithuanians, moved into the area, Pilsen remained a solidly Bohemian enclave until the middle of the 1950s, when Mexican immigrants began settling there. Today, Pilsen's population of about 45,000 is nearly 90% Hispanic.

"On January 26, 1946, the first official war bride contingent boarded the S.S. Argentina, a 20,600-ton Moore-McCormick liner which had transported over 200,000 troops during wartime. There were 452 brides, thirty of them pregnant; 173 children...The women had husbands in forty-five of the forty-eight states."

–Description of a historic sailing out of Southampton, England, from the book "War Brides."

PROLOGUE

"Five Minutes More," by Frank Sinatra of course, came from the jukebox in the hallway leading to the dank restrooms, although you could barely hear Frank's voice above the din.

She sat halfway down the long, scarred mahogany bar, a bottle of Bohemian and a glass on a coaster in front of her. The brown bottle was empty, the clear glass half full. She crossed her right leg saucily over her left, showing all calf and almost as much thigh. Good legs, enhanced by what were probably rayon stockings, given the scarcity of nylons in these early postwar days. The stool to her left was empty. He slid in.

"Mind if I take this seat?"

"I cannot honestly claim ownership of it," she sniffed, taking a drag on her cigarette and tossing her blonde hair in a gesture of indifference.

"You sound foreign. Like maybe...English?" He gave her what he had been told was an engaging grin.

"Well now, aren't you ever the clever one," she snapped, smirking. "Did you manage to work that out all by yourself?"

"I..." He didn't expect such a reaction, especially in a

neighborhood bar where a besotted conviviality was supposed to be the norm. But he had gotten rebuffed in saloons before, and he shifted to what had been successful in the past–the humble approach. "I'm sorry; I certainly didn't mean to be insulting. I really like your...your accent, whatever it is."

She raised an eyebrow. "I'm glad to hear that, yes I am. One very soon gets tired of people thinking that you're different." The trace of a smile creased a mouth generously coated with fiery red lipstick.

"But different can be good," he said with a deprecating nod, waving to the bartender. "Can I buy you a drink?"

"Only if it would make you feel good," she responded woodenly as "Zip-a-Dee-Doo-Dah" kicked in on the jukebox.

"Yes, it would make me feel good," he told her as he felt the sweat begin to percolate under his arms. He had entered territory where he didn't hold the high ground.

"The beer in this country is truly wretched," she pronounced, wrinkling her nose. "We wouldn't so much as touch this bilge back home."

He started to ask about "back home," but checked himself. One rebuff was enough for now. "What would you like?" he asked. "Name it."

"Scotch, a good Scotch–if they even have one here." She mashed her cigarette butt in a metal ashtray.

"What's your best Scotch?" he asked the bony,

sallow-faced bartender, who smoothly pivoted to the back of the bar, pulled down a bottle, and held it out for inspection.

She shrugged. "Suppose it will have to do. One can't be choosy now, can one?"

He ordered Scotch on the rocks for both of them and held out his pack of Chesterfields. She took one and he lit it, noting the thin silver band on her ring finger.

"Married?"

She nodded. "Sorry to say."

"Really? Why?"

"You don't want to hear my life story."

"Try me—I'm a good listener."

She took a sip of her drink. "Life doesn't always work out the way you think it will."

"Huh! I could write a book on that subject."

"You're married?"

"Divorced," he said, torching his own Chesterfield.

"At least you're free now, which is more than I can say for myself."

"What's stopping you...from getting divorced yourself, that is? There's all that red tape to go through, of course, but it's not illegal to split up. Or are you Catholic?"

She shook her head. "It's like admitting defeat. I came all the way across the bloody Atlantic for this." She turned her palms up and spread her arms, as if this gritty little bar on West 18th Street in Chicago's Pilsen neighborhood were the root of all her problems.

"What about your husband?"

She made a snorting sound. "What about him?"

"Is he treating you badly?"

"If you mean is he pinching every stinking penny we have until it squeals, yes, he damned well is. I haven't had a new pair of shoes since I came across the pond."

"Hey, Eddie, I gotta go now. See you tomorrow night, okay?" The speaker was a slender, chestnut-haired young woman with light blue eyes who was sitting on the other side of the blonde. He hadn't noticed her.

"Okay, I'll be here as usual, love," the blonde said.

"Friend of yours?" he asked after the brunette had clicked out into the night on her high heels.

"Marge? Yes, we both are here often. She's truly a good sort."

"What did she call you—Eddie?"

She laughed dryly. "Don't you go worrying yourself now, mate, I'm not a chap in ladies' togs. The name's Edwina. Not a common label here, but it is where I come from."

"It sounds much better than Eddie. So, what does your husband do?"

The song on the jukebox had ended, and before she could answer the question, one of the men along the bar called out to her: "Hey, Eddie, how 'bout you give us a song?"

She waved the request away. "Aw, you've heard me

enough in here, Len."

"No, no," he persisted. "Give us just one. How 'bout that 'White Cliffs of Dover' you do so well?" That brought cries of "Yes! Yes!" and applause from the saloon's denizens.

Eddie smiled and said, "Okay. Only the one song, though." She stood and started in with the familiar strains of the patriotic British World War II tune made famous by Vera Lynn:

There'll be blue birds over the White Cliffs of Dover;
Tomorrow just you wait and see...

When she had finished the full lyrics, the bar exploded in cheers. Eddie blew kisses all around and went back to her stool.

"That was wonderful," the visitor told her, meaning it. "You sound like a professional singer."

"I'd like to be," she said, flushed from the adulation. "Vera Lynn, the English star, she's my idol. I want to be able to sing that song like she does."

"Well, it sounds absolutely swell to me. Say, before you got up to sing, I started to ask about your husband. What does he do?"

She glared at the drink on the bar in front of her. "He mainly works, works, works. Always talking about overtime, and how we need money for a down payment on a house. Never mind me sitting at home alone every miserable night with nothing except the wireless–or the radio, as you Yanks like to call it–to keep me company.

But that was before I started coming in here. You might call this my freedom," she said, spreading her arms to encompass the bar.

She had seemed attractive to him when he strode into the bar, but the longer they talked, the less appealing and the more hard-boiled she appeared to become. He figured the scowl she wore had become frozen on her face.

"Well," he said, rising to leave, "I hope that everything works out between you and your husband."

"Not likely, Mate," she said over her shoulder as he turned toward the door. "I'd like to kill that bloody bastard."

CHAPTER 1

April 1946

"Seems like every day now there's another story about a ship loaded with war brides coming over here," Dirk O'Farrell of the *Chicago Sun* observed between slurps of coffee as he paged through his paper's final edition. "Wonder how all the good old American girls feel about these English and French and Dutch honeys, and even some *frauleins*, of all things, taking GIs off the marriage market. It doesn't seem quite right to me, somehow."

"And just how would you have stopped it, Dirk?" asked Packy Farmer of the *Herald American*, contemplating one of his misshapen little hand-rolled cigarettes before he lit it. "Put blinders on our soldiers when they're not on duty? Or maybe lock them in their barracks at night? You'd have had a full-scale revolt on your hands, I'll wager."

"True enough," O'Farrell answered. "There's no way of keeping nature from…well, from taking its course, shall we say. Not that all of our boys over there were exactly honest with the young ladies of Europe. You may remember a story a few weeks back–it was in your very own *Tribune*, Malek–about this girl over there, England I think, who fell for this soldier from North Carolina.

"He fed her this line about how he had a plantation back home. When she got there, she learned it was nothing but a shack deep in the backwoods, miles from civilization. She took one look, got the hell out of there, and grabbed the very next train up to New York. They found her later holed up in some Manhattan hotel, mad as hell."

"She ever go back to the guy?" Farmer asked.

"Story didn't say," O'Farrell answered, "but I'd lay eight to five that she ended up on a boat back to where she came from."

"What do *you* think, Snap?" Farmer posed, swiveling to face me. "You were over there toward the end. You must have seen lots of romances blooming between our boys and the local sweeties."

"Yeah, Malek," the sawed-off Eddie Metz of the *Times* piped up, after blowing his pathetic version of a smoke ring. "Even though you're married, I'll bet you had all kinds of chances to…you know."

"No, Eddie, I don't know," I shot back. "I wasn't there in uniform, as you damn well are aware; I was a correspondent for the *Tribune*. And my editors back here in Chicago didn't leave me a whole lot of time to go out on the town. They labored under some quaint theory that I was there to grind out copy, lots of it. I worked harder than I ever have."

"If that's your story, by all means, stick with it, Snap," O'Farrell said with a smirk. He leaned back and contemplated the peeling paint of indeterminate color on the ceiling. "No one on this side of the drink will ever be the wiser. What puzzles me, though, is why, after the paper brought you home from Europe, you actually asked to have your old beat back. I mean, you had all those bylines from England and Germany, and then you want to park yourself in this grimy dump with us again."

"It was just that I couldn't bear to be away from you fine fellows any longer," I deadpanned as they guffawed and groaned.

But Dirk O'Farrell had a point. For years, I had toiled as a police reporter for the *Chicago Tribune,* biggest of the city's five daily newspapers, in the pressroom at Police Headquarters, 1121 S. State St., Chicago, USA. Beginning shortly after Pearl Harbor, I had nagged various of the *Trib* editors to make me a foreign correspondent. Early in '45, not long after Catherine and I were married, they finally got tired of hearing me whine and sent me off to the paper's London bureau, where there was a temporary opening. Catherine stayed home, as it was clear I wouldn't be there for more than a few months.

It was an exciting, energizing time to be in England, along with all the other newspaper correspondents from across the country and around the world, to say nothing of the likes of Eric Sevareid and Edward R. Murrow. I even met Eisenhower twice and went to Berlin to cover the

Potsdam Conference where Truman, Stalin, and Churchill decided, for good or ill, on the shape postwar Europe would take. It was there, in mid-conference, that Clement Attlee, the Labor Party candidate who had defeated Churchill as prime minister in the summer election, took over Britain's seat at the table.

When I returned to Chicago late in '45, my stock at the paper was high, and I almost surely could have landed a spot as a general assignment reporter. But now that I was married again, I found I liked keeping regular hours, and the editors were happy to have me back in the Headquarters Press Room on the day shift.

I replaced a guy who was both lazy and incompetent, and who now works in public relations, writing florid press releases that extol, among other things, the gastronomic delights of dining at a chain of cut-rate steak houses in the city.

So here I was, back with the same crew that had been at Police Headquarters for a decade or longer—the aforementioned O'Farrell, Farmer, and Metz, plus Anson Masters of the *Daily News*.

"While we are on the subject of war brides, Mr. Malek," rumbled Masters, the dean of this press room corps, "I recall that you told us that a cousin of yours had married one."

"Ah, Anson, your memory still functions despite your advanced years," I told him. "Corporal Charlie Malek, late of our very own United States Army, has brought himself home a bride from England, name of Edwina. The couple is now ensconced in a four-room flat in that fine old Czech enclave of Pilsen, the very neighborhood where yours truly was himself born and reared."

"And they are happy, I presume?" Masters asked, running a hand over his bald and freckled pate.

"Moderately, as far as one can tell," I said, neglecting to mention that both Catherine and I had felt the tension between the couple on the two occasions we had been with them. In particular, Edwina had snapped at Charlie several times, usually because of his long working hours as a welder for the gas company.

My cousin, a quiet sort–some might go so far as to call him humble–pointed out to her that if they were to buy a house in the suburbs, they needed the money his overtime work brought in for the down payment.

"Well, Charles," she told him in a tone that seemed to be mimicking some British actress playing a duchess, "if having a house is more important to you than having a wife who is happy, then so be it. Sitting alone in an empty flat night after night is no lark for me, to that I can attest."

After they had left our place in Oak Park that night following a chicken dinner, Catherine shook her head in bewilderment. "What do you think of her, Steve?" she asked as she washed, and I dried, the dishes.

"The woman doesn't exactly hide her displeasure, does she? I wonder what kind of life she thought she was getting over here."

"Obviously not the kind she's got now. Did you see a lot of others like her in England who were anxious to come to this country?"

"Only one that I can recall offhand. I was in a pub near Russell Square in London one evening, standing alone at the bar with a pint, minding my own business. A little redhead, she couldn't have been more than five feet tall, was sitting with a girlfriend in a corner, bragging somewhat loudly about how she was going to be marrying this American pilot. 'We'll be living the high life,' she told her friend between puffs on a cigarette. 'His people, they're nobs, truly loaded. His Daddy owns some sort of business in Nebraska, what they call a drugstore over there, and I figure my Tommy will someday inherit it.'"

"'You are very lucky,' her friend said with a combination of awe and envy in her voice.

"The redhead nodded. 'I do feel fortunate,' she answered smugly. 'But don't you go fretting, dear; maybe you'll find yourself a nice, generous Yank, too. It's the only way to get out of this place, this life. I think we're all entitled to better times after what we've had to go through for these last six years.'"

Catherine dried her hands on a dishtowel and shook her head again. "That sounds like it could have been Edwina talking," she murmured. "I wonder how life has turned out for that redhead, especially if she found out that her father-in-law is only a small-town corner druggist in a tiny burg, and her husband is his only employee in the store."

"That's a very likely scenario," I agreed, "and the guy probably wants to spend the rest of his life in that little town smack in the middle of nowhere. Well, I don't blame these girls for wanting to come over here. Things are really tough in England right now–shortages of everything...food, clothes, housing, you name it. To say nothing of the bombed-out rubble and unexploded bombs, especially in London and the bigger industrial cities. It'll be years before they fully recover. I just hope things work themselves out between Charlie and Edwina."

"I do, too," Catherine said, her voice lacking the same conviction mine did.

CHAPTER 2

I was surprised at how quickly I slipped back into the routine at Police Headquarters after being away for the better part of a year. Of course, some of it was that my colleagues from the other papers welcomed me back warmly–but not simply out of the kindness of their black hearts.

Truth was, they needed me. In my previous years in the Headquarters pressroom, I had always covered the Detective Bureau at the request of my so-called competitors on the other dailies. Their reasoning was that, because the *Tribune* had the biggest news hole of any of the papers, I should be the one to have what was by far the most important beat in the building.

More to the point, because we all shared each other's news anyway, making a joke of the term 'competitive journalism,' everything I gleaned in my daily forays to the office of the chief of detectives would soon be theirs as well. And they didn't have to work to get it.

"Great to have you back, Snap," the *Herald American's* Packy Farmer said heartily on the morning of my return. "I'm sure you've got some great stories to tell."

"Well, I–"

"We'll want to hear those stories, of course," Farmer cut in, waving his cigarette, "but first to business. We've held open your old beat, of course. That clown, Mullaney, your bosses sent over here when you were away was totally worthless. He never spent more than a few minutes a day down in Fahey's office, and usually he didn't come back with crumbs." Farmer was referring to Chief of Detectives Fahey.

"Sorry to hear Mullaney wasn't up to your high standards of journalistic excellence, Packy," I said, noticing for the first time that he'd aged in my relatively short absence. His once-coal-black, brilliantined hair, which he parted in the center, now had a liberal dose of gray, as did the pencil-thin moustache that gave him the appearance of a riverboat gambler. But who was I to talk? Just that morning, while shaving, I took note of the growing infestation of gray in my own nondescript brown hair.

"Yeah, it's great to have you back, Malek," put in the lanky, lantern-jawed Dirk O'Farrell as he snapped his suspenders and lit up a Camel. "I second Packy's comment about Mullaney. I don't know what your bosses up in Tribune Tower could have been thinking when they sent that buzzard over here. He didn't seem to give a hoot about the job. Maybe he's better suited to writing press releases praising those leathery T-bones and filets at Leo's You-Pick-Em Steak Houses. By the way," Dirk went on, "this is the new City Press kid, Nick–don't know his last name."

There was a sixth desk in the pressroom, which belonged to whoever was the current reporter for the City News Bureau of Chicago, commonly known as City Press. It was a local police and courts reporting service used by radio stations and also by the newspapers for those stories they deemed not important enough to cover with their own people. City Press was basically staffed by young reporters starting out in the business, most of whom were rotated in and out of beats.

"Nice to meet you, Nick," I said, shaking hands with a short, stocky guy of about twenty-one with a blond crew cut and an earnest, open face. "Been here long?"

"Started two weeks ago," he said. "I just got out of the army–served in Italy for almost three years." He went on to tell me he was entering college on the G.I. Bill and would be taking night classes in the fall at the newly created University of Illinois campus at Navy Pier that had quickly been dubbed "Harvard on the Rocks."

"Well, good luck to you," I told him.

"Thanks," he said with a lopsided smile. "I've heard lots of good things about you from these guys. By the way, if you don't mind my asking, why do they call you Snap?"

"It's because he's addicted to snap-brim hats, like the one he wore in here this morning," Farmer drawled. "In your absence, we've filled Nick with all sorts of tales about what a bulldog you are, Snap. A credit to your profession, that's how we described you, proving that we can tell lies with the best of 'em. Hope you don't disappoint him, seeing that he's an impressionable lad and all."

"All right, now that we've established how good it is to have our Mr. Malek back," Anson Masters rumbled, "let's not forget that we all have work to do. Time to head for our beats."

As the senior man in this pressroom, Masters invariably took it upon himself to call a halt to the morning coffee-and-cigarettes bull sessions, which usually lasted the opening half hour or so of the workday.

On my first morning back, I walked down the well-worn single flight of marble steps to the office of the chief of detectives.

"Remember me?" I said, bowing at the waist to Elsie Dugo, who was hammering away at her ancient Smith Corona in the cramped anteroom outside the chief's office.

"Well, well, look who's come back from the wars," she cooed, clapping her hands and tilting her head. "I've always wanted to meet a foreign correspondent. This is so exciting. Where's your trench coat?"

"Now, try to control yourself, little lady. It's nice to see you again, too. The rumor mill tells me you've up and gotten yourself married while I was out of the country."

"'Tis true, sir," she chirped, waggling her ring finger at me so that the rock on it caught the light. "I knew you had done the very same thing yourself, so I thought, why not? Besides, a very fine gentleman by the name of Vincent Cascio swore that he couldn't live without me. So just what is a girl to do?"

"Precisely what you did," I grinned. "But is this Mr. Cascio prepared to keep you in the manner to which you would like to become accustomed?"

"How nice of you to inquire. The answer is yes, I believe he is. He's got a very good job with the Rock Island Railroad in their purchasing department. But I should ask you the same thing: Are you able to provide the new Mrs. Malek the kind of life that she surely deserves?"

"A fair question. I will do my utmost, of course, but part of that means I must perform admirably in my chosen profession. Which also means I must have access on a regular basis, including today, to the gentleman who oversees the detective operation of this vast and far-flung law enforcement agency. Can you help me with that challenging endeavor?"

"I will do my level best, as ever," she said with a wide smile, as she pushed the intercom button.

"Yeah?" came the growl from within.

"Old friend here to see you," she purred into the speaker.

"Got no old friends. Got no new ones, either. Hard to make friends in this damn business. Send 'im in, whoever it is."

I pushed through into the inner sanctum of Chief of Detectives Fergus Sean Fahey. "Nice to see you again, Fergus," I told him, tossing an unopened pack of Lucky Strikes onto his desk blotter.

"Well, I will be damned...I will be *God* damned," he mouthed, leaning back in his chair. "There was talk that you were in the States, and that you might even get your old job back."

"It's more than talk, Fergus. Here I am." I spread my arms wide and then dropped into one of his unmatched guest chairs. His desk was as I had last seen it...battered gunmetal gray, piled high with stacks of paper.

"I suppose you want some coffee," Fahey snapped.

"I thought you'd never offer. Is Elsie's brew still the best in the building?"

"Need you even ask?" he responded, pushing the buzzer on his desk. Within seconds, Elsie Dugo Cascio tripped in and placed a steaming mug in front of me. I smiled my thanks and got one in return before she left, closing the door behind her.

"One in a million," Fahey said. "I suppose you know she got married."

"So I just learned from her. Do you approve?"

"He's a damn good man from what I've seen of him. He'll take good care of her."

"Glad to hear it."

"I also understand via the grapevine that you've gone and gotten married yourself since the last time you were in here."

I nodded. "Just a few days before I got sent to Europe."

"Who's the–dare I say lucky–lady?"

"Of course she's lucky, Fergus. Name's Catherine. I've known her for years. She's the daughter of the late 'Steel Trap' Bascomb, whom I'm sure you remember."

"Damn right I do. He was one helluva reporter. I got to know him some way back when I was a patrolman working out of the Gresham District. I never understood why he stayed with City News all those years. He would've been the best police reporter on any of the dailies in this town."

"I agree. I think it had something to do with newspaper politics, as in 'let's not do anything to upset our almighty advertisers'."

"Huh! By the way, if you've known this Catherine for years, what took you so long, not that it's any of my business. You'd been divorced for what...ten years?"

"Pretty close to that, Fergus. Good question. I don't really have a good answer. I should have asked her to marry me at least three or four years earlier. Maybe I was afraid she'd say no."

Fahey nodded, ran a hand through his salt-and-pepper hair, and furrowed a ruddy brow. "Well, I suppose you're full of war stories. Do I have to listen to them?"

"Not at all," I replied amiably. "Try not to think of me as a recently returned war correspondent. Think of me instead as an intrepid reporter ready and eager to jump back into the fray in this great metropolis."

Fahey tore open the pack of Luckies and made a face. "Well, your stint as a correspondent hasn't toned down your language any. Actually, I'll probably regret these words in the none-too-distant future, but it's good to have you back."

"What a nice thing to say, Fergus. I'm touched at that, I really am."

"Well, don't put too fine a point on it," he muttered. He lighted up, then tossed the spent match into his ashtray. "Anything would be an improvement after that lackadaisical drip who took your place. He acted like he wished he was anyplace but here."

"So I understand from the boys upstairs. Well, he got his wish. He's a PR flak now, trying to get publicity for a string of cheap steakhouses."

Fahey nodded absently, and leaned back. "Yeah, maybe that will suit him better. He sure as hell wasn't cut out for this kind of work. He wandered in here every morning like he was in a trance, asked a few half-hearted questions about what was new, and then left. Masters and the others upstairs got so exasperated with him that they actually had to come down here themselves to find out what was going on."

"Poor bastards, what they've had to go through in my absence," I said. "You know the problem, Fergus? It was that I'd spoiled the whole bunch of them. They got used to my handing them everything all tied up neatly with a bow."

"Not that it means that much to me one way or the other, Snap, but that's what's wrong with your goddamn system," Fahey snarled. "You all share everything you get on your beats with each other. Whatever happened to those things that we used to call 'scoops' back in the old days?"

"Point taken, Fergus. Afraid, like with your question about Catherine, I don't have a ready answer except to say that it's been that way as long as I can remember, although admittedly I don't go back as far as you do."

"Well, I have to say that there are some equally nonsensical traditions in this department, but you can't quote me on that, of course."

"As indeed I won't, of course. On to business. Catch me up on what's been happening."

Fahey scowled. "Well, I suppose you know by now about that godawful Degnan murder. We're feeling a lot of heat on it and, as I'm sure you know, your own paper is offering ten grand for information about the killer." He was referring to the grisly murder and dismemberment of a six-year-old girl, in January.

"Yes, I do know about it, probably more than I want to. Any developments?"

He turned his palms up. "We keep hauling in suspects and following up leads, but so far, nothing. The Degnan killing is only part of it. We think the same guy also murdered two women last year. In the apartment of one of them, he wrote in lipstick on her mirror: 'For heaven's sake, catch me before I kill more.' We've got a madman on our hands, a real Jack the Ripper type. The whole city's up in arms about it."

"Hard to blame them. I hope he gets nailed soon. Then I read where that bookie, Richmond, got blown away by a shotgun right in front of his own house on Independence Boulevard a couple of days ago."

Fahey snorted and ground out his cigarette stub. "Well, if you read the reports, one thing's sure–it wasn't a robbery. He had more than eighteen hundred bucks on him in fives and tens, and he was wearing two diamond rings. It's got to be a revenge thing. Off the record, he's no great loss to the community, but that doesn't mean we won't do everything we can to find the triggerman."

"I would expect no less of you and your trusty legions, Fergus. Other than that, the unspeakable Degnan business, and the lipstick business, how are things generally?"

He shrugged. "I'm getting too old for this, Snap. Mary and I have a little cottage up in Wisconsin, not all that far over the Illinois line, and it's looking better to me all the time. It's nothing fancy, mind you, given my salary, but it's a comfortable place. I do some fishing and a little golfing when we're up there, and a lot of just plain sitting around loafing. I'd like to be spending more than just a couple weeks in the summer and a few other weekends there."

"You mean you're actually thinking of hanging it up? I can't imagine you dozing on the front porch of a log cabin tucked back in the woods someplace."

"Try harder. I do, every blessed day."

"Well, now that I'm back, maybe the job will become more stimulating for you."

"I can't imagine how."

Neither could I, but we both would soon find out.

CHAPTER 3

We had finished dinner and both were reading in the living room when the phone rang. Since I was nearer to the hallway where the instrument is kept, I got up to answer it.

My first thought was that it was my son Peter, calling from Champaign. Some kind of trouble, maybe.

It was trouble all right, but not Peter. "Stevie...Oh my God...Stevie!" The only person who called me that any more was my much-younger cousin Charlie, although I hardly recognized his voice, racked as it was with sobs and gasps.

"Charlie, what is it? Are you all right?"

"Edwina, oh, oh God." His words deteriorated into more sobbing or retching, I couldn't tell which.

"Charlie, tell me what's wrong! Where are you? Dammit, talk to me!"

"Home. She's in the living room...living room... knife. Oh Christ!"

I squeezed the receiver. "Charlie, listen to me! What's going on? Tell me."

"Edwina's on the sofa...in the living room...there's

blood...dead."

My mouth was so dry I could barely get the words out. "Charlie, listen. Have you called an ambulance?"

"Too late...too late." More sobbing.

"Are you absolutely sure she's dead?"

"Dead. Dead..."

"Charlie, call an ambulance, and call the police–do you hear me? I'm coming right over. Do you understand?"

I got a muffled response that might have been a "yes," and hung up.

"Steve, what's happened? What's going on?" Catherine had put her book down and risen, eyes wide with concern and a hand at her throat.

"I've got to get over to Charlie's place in Pilsen right away. It sounds like Edwina's been stabbed and maybe killed."

"Oh, no! Do you...want me to come with you?"

"No, stay here. I'll try to call you when I get there."

Five minutes later, I was backing our tired gray '39 Ford coupe out of the garage and into the alley. My watch read 7:20 p.m. as I wheeled out into Oak Park's dark, mostly empty streets in the only automobile I had ever owned. We had bought it from a used-car dealer on Madison Street just after I got back from Europe, and I was now teaching Catherine how to drive, only weeks after I had taught myself.

I drove east, back through the years, to Pilsen, the

Chicago neighborhood where I was born and where I spent the first twenty years of my life. Like so many of the residents, we–my parents, my sister, and I–lived in a three-story building that contained about two dozen apartments. Ours, with parlor, dining room, kitchen, three bedrooms, and a rickety wooden back porch, was on the top floor.

About once every three weeks, my father reminded all of us how lucky we were to live in one of the few three-bedroom flats in the building. At least five of the boys in my grade school class at St. Agnes shared a bedroom with two or more siblings, and Robert Benes slept in the same room with two brothers and two sisters.

Pilsen was heavily Czech, which is to say Bohemian, although we had some Polish families and a substantial number of Slovaks in the neighborhood as well–the latter a group that my aged grandmother had looked upon with disdain. When, as an eight-year-old, I asked her why she didn't like Slovaks, she merely said, "Because we (meaning people hailing from Bohemia) are better than they are." The way she spoke made it clear that there was nothing more to be said on the subject.

My father worked his whole adult life as a streetcar motorman. We never had a lot of money, but neither did anyone else in the neighborhood, so I never felt deprived. I hung out with a group of boys my own age, and the worst trouble we ever got into was shoplifting candy from old Mr. Havlicek's corner store at 16th and Laflin. When my parents found out, thanks to a tattletale named Louie Janak, my pal Freddie and I had had to wash the store's windows, inside and out, once a week for two months.

My father's brother, Uncle Frank, and his wife, Aunt Edna, lived just two blocks from us in a four-room flat over a grocery store–not Mr. Havlicek's. When I was fourteen, my cousin Charlie, their only child, was born. By the time he was two, Aunt Edna, who was a demanding, domineering sort, was bringing him over to our flat and telling my mother that "Maybe Stevie can watch him and play with him." So it was that I got stuck with little Charlie with increasing frequency for the next two or three years and often ended up having to drag him along when I played baseball or football on the vacant lots or in the little park near where we lived.

As Charlie got older and I moved off into the work world, I, of course, saw less of him. But even the occasional family holiday gatherings were enough for me to see that he was growing into a withdrawn and somewhat unassertive kid who tended to retreat into himself, no doubt because of his imperious mother. This passive, meek nature stayed with him into adulthood, which made me wonder how he could have survived the rigors of the military, although he apparently acquitted himself well as a soldier in the Italian campaign.

I pulled up in front of the brick three-flat just a few doors from 18th Street, where Charlie and Edwina lived. There was neither a police cruiser nor an ambulance in front of the building. I pressed the button for Charlie's second-floor apartment and, after a wait of about 30 seconds, got buzzed in.

When I reached their landing one flight up, Charlie Malek, twenty-eight and looking older, stood in the doorway, eyes glazed and watery, mouth agape, head shaking almost convulsively.

"She's...there, Stevie," he said motioning with his head and stepping aside as I entered the living room.

She was there, all right, sprawled on the lumpy brown sofa, arms spread, hands clenched, and with her flowered green dress hiked up slightly but not obscenely. Her stockinged legs were stiffly straight, and one shoe was off, laying several feet away on the floor. Her eyes and mouth were open, her face frozen in a rictus of terror.

The reason for it all was a kitchen knife, half-buried in her left breast. A bloodstain had spread so that it covered the entire front of her dress as well as the sofa cushion.

I sucked in air. "You didn't call an ambulance or the police?"

Charlie shook his head dumbly. "I could see she was dead, Stevie."

"Okay, dammit, but you've still got to make the calls, especially to the cops," I barked, kneeling and placing my fingers on her carotid, confirming my cousin's diagnosis. "Is this how you found her?"

He nodded. "Uh-huh. When I came home tonight

after work, I opened the door, and..."

"Was the door locked?" I asked, moving toward the telephone on a table in the hall.

Charlie shook his head. "That surprised me. Sometimes she was, uh...out when I got home, but even when she was here, she always kept the door locked."

"Don't you usually work a lot later than this?" I asked, looking at my watch.

"Yeah, I do. We were supposed to be working on a new gas line down in Englewood tonight, but the pipe never got delivered by the manufacturer, so our whole crew was sent home."

I dialed the central police number, telling the voice at the other end that a body had been found at the address in Pilsen, second-floor apartment. When the voice started asking questions, I cradled the receiver.

"Okay, Charlie, the police'll be here in minutes, and chances are that then you'll be in a whole lot of trouble."

"But this is how I found her!" he keened, gesturing shakily toward his wife's body.

"Can you prove it?"

"Well, no, but..."

"What about your neighbors? They must have heard something."

"The first-floor apartment is vacant and the people above us, the Zaceks, are out of town, visiting friends someplace over in Indiana, I think."

I grimaced. "Convenient. Look, Charlie, unless I'm

very wrong, I believe you and Edwina have done your share of quarreling. I've been around the two of you just enough to get that sense. Chances are likely that when your neighbors have been at home, they've heard you, so whatever you do, don't tell the cops that you never spoke a harsh word to each other. They'll quickly find out otherwise."

Charlie started to retch and I rushed him toward the bathroom, shoved him inside, and closed the door as he began vomiting.

I called to tell Catherine I was at Charlie's and briefly filled her in, but had to hang up when the doorbell rang. The police had arrived and I buzzed them in.

I all but dragged an ashen-faced Charlie back out of the bathroom and propelled him to the living room. "Let them in before they knock the damn thing off its hinges," I said sharply.

He swung the door open to a pair of grim-faced, square-jawed patrolmen who looked capable of anchoring the interior of the Bears' defensive line.

"You the one who made the phone call?" one grunted through clenched teeth.

I had told Charlie to say that he was the caller, and he nodded "yes" while doing a clumsy backward shuffle as they tromped into the room like advancing infantrymen without bayonets. Both of them put on the brakes when they saw Edwina's body.

"Ambulance's on the way," the tight-lipped one said,

although it was clear from his expression that he knew she was beyond earthly help. "What's the story? You live here?"

Charlie nodded again, wide-eyed and gulping.

"Name?"

He stammered his name.

The cop–his badge read Brady–inclined his head toward the body. "Who's she?"

"My wife…Edwina…Malek."

He snarled in my direction. "And who're you?"

Before I could answer, two medics and a pair of plainclothes detectives burst into the room, suggesting that the patrolmen must have propped open the foyer door downstairs. If anybody else tried had to squeeze into the room, we'd have been in violation of the fire code. The medics went straight to the body while the taller of the two detectives, a curly-haired specimen with a broken nose, huddled with Brady as they both looked in our direction.

"You?" the detective gruffed at me, obviously expecting a response.

"I'm his cousin, Steve Malek," I said. "Charlie called me when he found…found her."

"Why didn't you call *us* first?" the detective growled at Charlie.

My cousin went through a shrugging motion and shook his head.

"All right," he sighed, pulling out a notebook and

flashing his badge. "My name's Prentiss, detective bureau. This is Hodge," he said, indicating his partner, a balding, porky guy with ruddy cheeks and a permanent frown who also flashed his badge.

As this was going on, the medics had knelt beside Edwina's body. One looked up at Prentiss, shaking his head. There was no mistaking the message.

"All right, Mr. Malek," Prentiss said to Charlie, pen poised over notebook. "Is this your doing?"

"No. I–"

The detective sneered at him. "You know she's dead, and I think you also know how she got that way. It would be–"

"Wait a minute!" It was my turn to interrupt. "Give the man a chance to answer."

"We'll get to you soon enough, cousin," Prentiss spat heatedly.

A surge of anger overtook me. "Just so you know, Detective, I'm a *Tribune* reporter, based at 11th and State. I meet with Chief Fahey every morning." I pulled out my police press card and held it up in front of his face.

Prentiss flushed. "Are you by any chance threatening me, chum?"

"Not at all, but since you were showing your credentials, I felt you ought to see mine, too."

"Well, thank you so very goddamn much, *sir*," Prentiss hissed, turning to his partner. "Dave, take our Mr. Very Important Reporter here someplace, maybe the kitchen. See what you can find out from him about what went on in here tonight, and don't let him give you any lip. My experience with reporters is that they've all got smart mouths to go with their small brains."

Detective Hodge nodded and gestured in the direction of the hall. I followed him to the small kitchen, where we sat at the Formica-topped, chrome-edged table.

"Jack, he's got a kind of short fuse," the stocky cop said by way of an apology for his partner. "He thought you was tryin' to show him up in there."

"Not my intent," I replied evenly, "but I thought it was best that you both ought to know who I am in addition to being Charlie's cousin."

Hodge nodded, pulled a notebook from an inside pocket of his rumpled gray suit coat, and propped his elbows on the table. "Good idea. Now, if you can tell us exactly what happened tonight."

I recited chapter and verse from Charlie's call to me until the moment the cops entered his apartment, with one exception: I said it was Charlie who phoned the police. He was already in enough trouble.

"Did you know his wife?" the ever-frowning Hodge asked.

"Yes, a little. They'd been married for less than a year. She was a war bride, from England. She came over here with a whole boatload of others like her."

"Lotta them here now, sure enough. How did they get along?"

I tried to make my shrug looked offhanded. "I didn't see them all that often, but they were like all married couples, I suppose. Mostly good times, but the occasional bumpy spot. You probably know how that is."

He nodded soberly. "Oh, yeah, that I do. Did you ever hear or see anything that made you think he'd want to...well, do anything violent?"

I shook my head. "My cousin is the last person I know who would get violent. He's probably the mildest, meekest guy I've ever known."

Hodge contemplated his notebook. "Back to the wife. How would you describe her personality?"

"I'd say she was the fun-loving type–wanted to go out to movies, restaurants, dancing, that sort of thing. I guess that's understandable, given how tough things were in England during the war. There wasn't much fun to be found there."

"Uh-huh, so I heard. My brother was stationed near London for two years. Did the two of them go out on the town much?"

"I don't think so. We had them over for dinner at our place in Oak Park a couple of times, but Charlie had been working a lot of overtime. He was trying to get money to buy a house out in the suburbs."

"Like a lotta people these days," Hodge said. "So, did the wife sit around at home nights?"

"I really don't know," I said truthfully.

"Seems that life could get awful lonesome alone in

the flat every night," the thickset detective observed.

"I suppose so," I agreed.

"Do you know if they had any other friends...maybe neighbors they got together with?"

"It's possible, although Charlie never mentioned anyone to me." That was also true.

Hodge scribbled something in his notebook and, if I read him right, he was trying to come up with another line of questioning. As it turned out, he didn't have to. Before he could open his mouth, his belligerent partner barreled into the kitchen.

"Find out anything from him, Dave?" Detective Jack Prentiss barked from just inside the doorway, gesturing in my direction with a thumb.

"Well, I haven't really—"

"Never mind. We're taking Malek in for more questioning."

Hodge's broad face registered puzzlement. "Which Malek?"

"The one whose wife is dead, of course," Prentiss said derisively. "We'll worry about the newspaper guy here later." He looked down at me as though I were a form of life somewhere below a tadpole and slightly above a worm.

"Does that mean that Charlie's under arrest?" I asked.

Prentiss leered at me. "Figure it out for yourself, scribbler. And feel free to whine to the bosses over at 11th and State all you want to. Now get the hell out of here. I can't stand the stench that a reporter gives off, it makes me want to puke."

"What's your partner's beef with the newspapers?" I asked after Prentiss had stormed out. "Did we queer one of his cases?"

Hodge turned a palm up. "Beats me," he said, "but Jack's had that attitude as long as I've known him, which is going on six years now."

"Sorry to hear it, but most of us didn't get into this business to win a popularity contest."

"Same with our line of work," the detective said. "I've been called a whole lotta names, most of which you couldn't print in your newspaper. Ya gotta grow a thick skin."

I smiled ruefully. "So I guess both of us got into our respective lines of work for the glory, huh?"

That got the hint of a smile from the dour Hodge. "Yeah, that and the fabulous pay, of course."

"Oh, of course; how could I have forgotten that wonderful benefit of the job? Well, I think I'd better check on my cousin before you haul him away. Think you can keep Prentiss from taking a swing at me?"

"Aw, his bark is worse–"

"Than his bite, I know, I know," I said over my shoulder as we walked back down the hall to the living room. Edwina's body was gone now, and so were the patrolmen and the medics. The medical examiner and his crew, who must have come in while I was in the kitchen with Hodge, were packing up their gear. Charlie sat hunched on an easy chair in one corner with his head in his hands as Prentiss flipped his notebook closed and slid it into a pocket.

"Alright, let's go," he said coldly, tapping Charlie on the shoulder.

"So, are you booking him or not?" I asked. No copper, uniformed or otherwise, was going to intimidate me, especially where a relative was involved.

Prentiss pivoted toward me, meaty fists balled. "Go to hell, newshound."

"Can I quote you on that for our late editions, Detective Prentiss?"

"Damn right. Can you spell my name, or do I have to write it down for you?"

"Thanks, but don't bother. I wouldn't trust you to get the letters in the proper order."

"Why, you miserable bastard, I'll–"

"Don't, Jack. Take it easy." Prentiss looked like he was going to haul off and swing at me, but Hodge wrapped burly arms around his partner, pulling him back.

"Charlie, are you okay?" I asked as though we were the only two in the room.

He looked up at me through teary eyes and nodded numbly.

"You sure?"

He nodded again. "Thanks, Stevie," he mumbled. "I think they…they want me to go with them."

"Yeah. Well, don't worry; I'll be checking on you. And I will look into getting you a lawyer."

Prentiss snorted. "Sure, your cousin here, the hotshot, know-it-all reporter, will try to start pulling strings for you. Must be nice to have friends way up there in high places. If you want to call the newspaper racket a high place, that is. To me, it's about as low as you can get without climbing into a manhole and wading through the sewer slime."

I started to fire back at him, but stifled it. At this moment, in this place, there was nothing I could do to help Charlie except beat a retreat and regroup. Which I did.

CHAPTER 4

I logged barely five hours sleep that night. After I got home, Catherine and I went over what had occurred in Pilsen until well past 1:00 a.m.

"What do you think's going to happen to him?" she asked as she poured both of us a cup of newly brewed coffee at the kitchen table.

"Damn, I wish I could tell you. I don't know enough about Edwina to hazard a guess as to who she knew in Chicago, if anybody. It could have been a break-in, but that won't help Charlie if there are no fingerprints or any other evidence."

Catherine gave an involuntary shudder.

"On top of that, they'd apparently had their share of quarrels, and chances are the neighbors would have overheard them. In those old neighborhoods, the walls have ears, as they say. It's only a matter of days, or maybe just hours, before the cops find one or more of these neighbors who will be more than willing to talk about the exchange of angry words between spouses, one of whom is now deceased."

"I'm so terribly, terribly sorry about what's

happened," she said, leaning over to squeeze my arm. "But I'm also concerned about you. How are you going to cover this for the *Tribune*? Or can you?"

"As usual, my love, you ask excellent questions– hardly surprising given the newspaper genes that run in your family. And I don't have a ready answer, except that of course I'll have to make my editors aware of the situation. Actually, it's possible that the story is already out, depending on whether that surly detective Prentiss has filed his report. I'll know soon enough."

I walked into the Headquarters pressroom a few minutes before nine the next morning, unsure of what awaited me. The first hint that the murder hadn't yet been reported came when our overnight man, Corcoran, told me what a quiet night it had been. "Which is just fine as far as I'm concerned," he said, turning the *Trib* desk over to me and donning his rumpled suit coat. If Corcoran wasn't the laziest reporter on the paper, he definitely ranked in the top three, especially now that Mullaney had joined the ranks of press agents.

The other members of the dayside crew began drifting in, first Farmer, then Metz, and Nick, the City News kid. I didn't even wait for the others to show up. I had very early business on the floor below.

"Good morning," Elsie Dugo Cascio said with uncharacteristic reserve as I walked into her small office area. "Go right on in, he's expecting you." Another departure from the norm.

I pushed open the door to Fergus Fahey's office. He looked up, giving me a perfunctory nod. "It won't surprise you, of course, to learn that I've been expecting you," he said.

"No," I told him, "I'm not surprised." I eased into one of his guest chairs just as Elsie placed a mug of coffee in front of me. I smiled my thanks.

"Tough night," Fahey said, running a hand through his graying hair. "Want to talk?"

"You go first."

He grunted and picked up some sheets, holding them at arm's length. "This is Prentiss's report. I suppose you know much of what's in it."

"I probably do. Try me."

"I'll just hit the high spots: 'Edwina Moreland Malek...age twenty-four, native of Great Britain...died from a single stab wound to the heart inflicted by a kitchen knife. Estimated time of death, six to seven P.M...Husband, Charles Edward Malek, age twenty-eight, Chicago native, army veteran. Couple known by neighbors to have quarreled, sometimes loudly, particularly the wife. Charles Malek booked and charged with the murder, being held without bond in the Bridewell...The suspect's cousin, Steven Malek, *Chicago Tribune* reporter assigned to police headquarters, attempted to intimidate the investigators.'" Fahey put the paper down on his desk. "Want me to go on, or have you heard enough?"

"Your Detective Prentiss is a twenty-four carat, gold-plated prick. And that's just for starters. Wait till I get warmed up on the subject."

Fahey came forward in his chair, jaw set. "I won't debate that point with you, Snap, except to say that Jack Prentiss has had problems with the working press for a long time now. Some years back, a reporter on the *Daily News*, I believe it was, misquoted him badly and got him in trouble with some of his higher-ups in the department—not me, mind you. He was on the uniformed force back then. But he's been a damn good dick for us. He was all over the area last night, knocking on doors; and he found two neighbors who claim that your cousin and his wife had had more than a few screaming matches.

"Anyway, so much for that. Now, I've suppressed this report, waiting for you to show up today. And I—"

I took a sip of Elsie's coffee. "Why no bail for Charlie?"

"The heat is really on since the Degnan murder," Fahey answered. "Every time there's a female murdered now, the presumption is that it's the same guy who killed Suzanne Degnan, as well as those two women who were butchered in their apartments last year."

"Dammit, Charlie couldn't have killed anybody, Fergus."

The chief of detectives looked at the ceiling, as if seeking guidance from on high. "How well do you really know your cousin, Snap?"

"Well enough to know that he couldn't have done this. He practically redefines the word 'meek'."

"Not according to those neighbors Prentiss talked to."

"I'll bet that if you go deeper into those so-called screaming matches that your man Prentiss dug up, you'll find that Edwina did most, if not all, of the screaming."

"And just why might that be?"

I drank more coffee before responding. "Based on what I saw during our few meetings, Edwina seemed to think she should be living a better, richer life than she was. She could be pretty rough on Charlie."

Fahey lit a cigarette and looked at me through narrowed eyes. "So, she was unhappy with her lot here, right?"

"I think she felt things over on this side of the Atlantic would somehow be, well...cushier, more luxurious, I guess. It seems that a lot of people from outside the good ol' USA think we have it better than we really do."

"It's still the best place in the world to be living," Fahey growled as if daring contradiction.

"You won't get an argument from me on that, Fergus."

"So, we're agreed on something, but now what? Do you want to take this report up to your colleagues in the pressroom? Or would you rather tell one of them to come down here and handle it?"

"Shit, I can't do that, Fergus, and you know it. Mind if I use your phone?"

He threw up his hands. "Why not? Once the camel gets his nose under the tent, etc. Want to park yourself in my chair, too?"

I ignored him and dialed the *Trib* city desk, asking for Murray, the day city editor and a first-class newsman.

"Hal, it's Malek. I've got a problem here."

"So, what's new about that?"

"Hear me out. There's been a murder in Pilsen—my cousin Charlie's wife, a war bride from England. He's been charged, and they're holding him without bond. Would you feel more comfortable having another man cover it?"

"Huh! Now why would I want to do that?"

"I don't know. I suppose because somebody in the Tower might think I wouldn't be objective."

Murray snorted. "How do you feel? *Can* you be objective?"

"I like to think so."

"Hell, I do, too, Snap. But I'll check with the higher-ups anyway. If somebody has a problem, you'll be the second to know. In the meantime, stay on the story. What time did the murder happen?"

"Around six or seven last night."

"Damn. If we'd known earlier, we could have got something in the three-star final. Now the P.M.'s are going to get the jump on us."

"Um, there's something else you need to know, Hal."

"Yeah?"

"I was there last night, at my cousin's place in Pilsen, that is. He phoned me after he came home and found his wife dead, stabbed."

"And you didn't call it in to the desk?"

"No, I didn't."

Through the receiver, I could hear Murray exhaling, not once but twice. "So...a case of family ahead of job, right?"

"Well, I..."

"Same call I probably would have made in your shoes," he said stiffly. "But for God's sakes, file something in time for the early editions, okay?"

I cradled Fahey's phone and turned to him. "All right, let's go over this again. I've got editors at the *Trib* and a bunch of so-called reporters one floor up who I'm supposed to keep happy. Nobody ever said that life was going to be easy."

A half hour later, I strode back into the pressroom to find that all of them were at their desks. I felt like I had interrupted a conversation, the way they all clammed up and looked at me.

"Ah, Mr. Malek, what do you bring from the eminent Chief Fahey?" Masters asked, keeping his tone neutral.

"I think you know, Anson," I said, "the way word gets around this building. But I know you'll all want the official version, so here it is:

"Last night about 7:00 or 7:30 p.m., Charles Malek, war veteran, age twenty-eight–and yes, he's my cousin, although I doubt that will interest the readers of your respective papers–arrived at his apartment in Pilsen (I gave the address) to find his wife, Edwina, his British war bride of less than one year, sprawled dead on the living room sofa with a knife embedded in her chest." I paused. The room had grown as quiet as a mortuary.

"Malek had been working at his job as a gas company welder, as was usually the case, and said he found the body when he got home. He phoned me in a panic, and when I arrived at the scene, I insisted that he call the police. They arrived soon after, as did the medical people.

"The police learned from neighbors that the couple had quarreled often. The dead woman seemed unhappy that her husband worked such long hours, leaving her at home alone. Malek was booked and is being held without bail in the Bridewell. Any questions?"

Dirk O'Farrell whistled. "Not often that we get a first-hand description of a murder scene. I for one am not going to include your visit to the apartment when I file, Snap. No sense in mentioning the competition on our pages. Again, how long did you say they'd been married?"

"A little less than a year," I answered.

"Did you know her, Snap?" Eddie Metz asked.

"Not very well. Met her a couple of times, that's all." I wasn't about to discuss her personality.

"Got any thoughts as to what happened?" Packy

Farmer put in.

I shook my head. "Not a clue, except to say that my cousin seemed like the last guy who would do something like this. He's as gentle as a puppy. I know that it was someone else, no question."

That got sympathetic nods all around. "Why no bail for your cousin–the Degnan business and those other murders?" Farmer posed.

"Yeah, or so Fahey tells me. Until they catch that perverted moron, every murdered girl or woman in the city will be seen as another potential victim. Each of our papers, the Crime Commission, and every reformer around, all of them are applying the heat. Hell, Fahey looks like he's aging by the hour."

"He's not alone," Anson Masters said. "All the other high-ranking cops are feeling the pressure as well. Your cousin have a lawyer?"

"No, and that's something I've got to work on. Charlie wouldn't know where to begin looking."

"Since Clarence Darrow's been dead these several years now, my suggestion would be McCafferty," Masters volunteered. "That's who I'd want on my side if I were in a spot like this."

He was referring to Liam McCafferty, known popularly in the Chicago press and the legal community as the "Irish Pericles" for his spirited and emotional orations in the defense of his clients.

It was said that he once had nine of the twelve jurors

simultaneously in tears as he extolled the character and virtues of a man on trial as a mass murderer. Not surprisingly, the defendant was acquitted. Also not surprisingly, no one else was ever charged with the crime.

"Good suggestion, Anson, thanks. I'll definitely look up McCafferty. But first, I'd like to see my cousin in the Bridewell. I'm going to take an extended lunch break, probably be gone a couple of hours. Can someone cover for me?"

"Consider it done, Snap old man," O'Farrell said, leaning back with his feet on his desk and blowing a series of well-rounded smoke rings ceilingward. "You've covered for me more than a few times, as I recall, and I'm happy to return the favor. If any of your editors call one of us looking for you, we'll just tell 'em you're closeted with Fahey trying to wring some information out of that stubborn old Irishman."

"Better go easy on the stubborn Irishman bit, though," I told him with a smile. "The person most likely to call from our city room is another son of the Old Sod, Hal Murray, who might take umbrage at that phrase. See you all later."

CHAPTER 5

It was raining steadily as I stepped out of a Checker cab and approached the high, gray walls of the city jail at 26th and California on the southwest side of town. Popularly known as the Bridewell, the place had been named, or so I was told, after a notorious London penitentiary of earlier times.

The inside was, if anything, even drearier than the exterior. I had been there only once before, about half a dozen years back, interviewing the then-warden for a Sunday feature on the inner workings and day-to-day operation of a municipal prison.

"I'm here to see Charles Malek," I told the thick-necked, uniformed guard who was seated behind a counter in the entrance hall. He looked up from a well-thumbed copy of *Black Mask* magazine, the cover illustration of which showed a curvy, leggy blonde wearing a red dress, high heels, and a terrified expression, being carried off by a sneering, shadowy man in a fedora who seemed intent on inflicting some sort of bodily harm upon the comely lady.

"Your name?" he asked in a bored tone, his eyes

never leaving the magazine page.

"Also Malek–Steven Malek. I'm his cousin."

"Identification?"

I pulled out my police press card, which he glanced at without expression or apparent interest. "*Trib* reporter, eh?"

"Yes."

"Must be tough, havin' a relative in here, huh?"

"Tougher on him. He'd rather be somewhere else," I said evenly.

"So would they all, buddy." He rifled through a sheaf of papers on the counter, running his thick index finger down the list of names.

"Here he is, cell block B. See that hall on your left? Take it until you get to the barred doors and tell the guard there who you want to see. He'll fix you up," he said, turning his attention back to the apparently riveting pages of *Black Mask*.

I thanked him and walked down a hall with a concrete floor, concrete walls, and a concrete ceiling, all in a shade of gray that more or less matched the outer walls. What lighting there was came from low-wattage bulbs in metal mesh ceiling fixtures spaced every twenty feet or so.

At the barred doors, another uniform considered me without enthusiasm. "Yeah?" he asked, or at least I assumed there was a question mark after the word.

"I'm here to visit Charles Malek. I'm his cousin Steve. Same last name. Guy up front sent me back."

"Lemme check to see if he's in his cell." He turned a corner and disappeared, the ring of keys on his broad hip jangling.

After about a minute, he returned and swung open the bars. "Down the hall to the visitors' room, first door on the left. He should be there by now. You've got ten minutes with him. The guard in there'll tell you when your time's up."

The room was long, narrow, and windowless, divided down the middle by a steel partition about four feet high. At intervals, there were screened openings in the partitions and chairs on both sides of them. At the fourth opening down, on the prisoners' side of course, sat Charlie Malek in light brown inmates' garb, looking dazed.

"Hi, Stevie," he said, trying without success to form a smile. "Hey, thanks a lot for coming by."

I dropped into my chair and looked around. A guard, his back against the wall, stood about ten feet from me. Charlie and I were the only other people in the room. "How are you holding up?" I asked, realizing as I said it how stupid the question must have sounded.

He shrugged. "The food's actually not bad. The guards are surly, especially the one who thinks I killed that poor Degnan girl. One good thing–I've got a cell all to myself."

"Likely for your own protection. Have you done anything about getting a lawyer?"

"Uh, no. They asked me if I had an attorney and I said

I didn't. I was told I could get myself a public defender."

"Screw that. You'll need better counsel, no offense to the defender's office. I'm going to try to get you the best criminal lawyer in town–named McCafferty."

Charlie shook his head. "Thanks anyway, Stevie, but I can't begin to afford some big-shot like him."

"Don't worry," I said in a low voice, leaning forward. "It'll be covered."

"I can't let you pay all that, Stevie," he said, also lowering his voice. "You're not exactly a Rockefeller."

"Thanks for reminding me, but like I said, don't worry. I'll give you plenty of opportunity to pay me back later. Count on it. The big thing now is to get you somebody good and get you the hell out of this mess."

"I…thanks, thanks a lot."

"Now Charlie, I need to know more about what Edwina did nights when you were out working your tail off for the grand old gas company. Did she have some place, or places, where she liked to go?"

He ran a hand through dusty-brown hair and swallowed hard, making the Adam's apple in his skinny neck bob up and down like a yo-yo. "Well, I know that in the last few weeks–or maybe it's been longer–she'd taken to dropping in at Horvath's Tap pretty regular."

"Oh, yeah, I remember it, although I don't think I've ever been in there. It's that joint on 18th at around Marshfield, right?"

"Yes, that's the place all right. And like you, I've

never been in there. It's been around for years, though, ever since I can remember. It might have opened right after Repeal. I think my dad stopped in occasionally."

"Edwina make some friends there?"

"I don't know. I suppose she could have. She could be very social, as you know. Liked to be out and around the town. Wanted to be around people."

"Did she ever mention anyone specifically?"

He shook his head. "I don't think so, at least not to me."

"Was she home when you got home from work?"

"Sometimes. I usually put in another four or five hours of overtime after the day shift ended, which got me home by nine-thirty or ten most days. About half the time, she was there when I came in."

"And the other half?"

He smiled ruefully. "Sometimes, she wouldn't be back till, oh, eleven or even twelve."

"Didn't that bother you, Charlie?"

"Sure, but then you know Edwina. She is–was–very headstrong."

"And she was always at Horvath's?"

"Yeah, as far as I know. She told me it was such a friendly place. Said it reminded her of some of the pubs back home, even though the beer wasn't as good. She complained a lot about that. I told her it didn't seem proper for a married woman to be going into bars by herself, but she just laughed and called me an old-fashioned boy."

"Did you ever go in there with her?"

"No, I never did. I probably should have, but I was always…"

"Afraid of what you'd find?" I put in.

He gnawed at a fingernail. "I guess, maybe. Or maybe she'd think I was spying on her. Edwina had quite a temper."

"I got that impression the few times I saw her. Anything else you can tell me that might point us to what happened?"

"No…no. The way I figure it, somebody followed her home and forced his way into the apartment. Then he must have…tried to…" Charlie began to sob quietly, and I looked around at the guard. He wasn't paying any attention to us.

"Okay, I'm going to talk to McCafferty, that lawyer I mentioned," I told him, "and I'm also going to pay a visit to Horvath's. I'll try to stop by again in the next few days, okay?"

"Okay, Stevie. And thanks," he said, sniffling and dabbing his eyes.

When I got back to the pressroom late that afternoon, they all looked questioningly at me, but nobody said anything, which I appreciated. For all the carping I've done about this crew over the years, on balance they're a decent sort.

First thing the next morning, back at Headquarters, I

looked up Liam McCafferty's office on LaSalle Street and dialed his number. A crisply efficient, but pleasant, feminine voice answered and I gave her my name, adding that I was a *Tribune* reporter based at 11th and State.

"May I tell Mr. McCafferty what this is about?"

"I'm afraid not. It's a very sensitive subject," I replied in what I hoped was a conspiratorial tone.

"Can you be more specific, sir?"

"I'm afraid I can't. But I know that Mr. McCafferty will definitely want to talk to me."

"Very well. Hold the line please." The voice had become distinctly less pleasant.

I waited for what seemed like three minutes, but probably was less, before I heard a voice laced with brogue say "McCafferty here."

"This is Steve Malek of the *Tribune*. You may be aware that there was a murder in Pilsen the night before last."

"I read the newspapers, including yours, Mr. Malek. They all had the story with varying degrees of detail, the afternoon editions yesterday, the morning ones today." His tone was businesslike, but not unfriendly.

"You may also be aware that the man being held is named Malek."

"And why do you suppose that I picked up my telephone?" he replied with a slight chuckle. I liked the sound of his voice.

"Okay, so you're on to me. Charlie Malek is my

cousin, and I want you to defend him."

"I do not come cheap, Mr. Malek."

"And I do not pay cheap, Mr. McCafferty." Brave words from one who had no idea what kind of dollars were involved.

"Well put, sir, well put indeed. I gather from the news reports that your cousin is in the Bridewell. Foul place. Never liked it. Should be torn down like the Bastille was. I just finished a case two days ago, so your timing is excellent. I shall endeavor to pay a visit to him today."

"Thank you," I said, giving him my phone numbers in the pressroom and at home. I was pleased that the great lawyer had agreed to take Charlie on, but I also knew that my being with the *Tribune* was a factor.

Talk around town was that, second only to money, the silver-haired, glib Liam McCafferty craved publicity, mountains of it. And the *Tribune* was printed on mountains of paper, a million copies a day, and even more on Sundays.

CHAPTER 6

That evening, as usual, I went over the day's activities with Catherine at dinner, concentrating on my visit to Charlie in jail as well as my hiring of Liam McCafferty.

"It looks bad for him, doesn't it, Steve?" she asked, the concern evident in her voice.

I nodded. "You and I could tell from the very first that theirs was not a marriage made in heaven, or anyplace resembling it. Unfortunately for Charlie, several of their fellow residents of Pilsen know the same thing, as the cops quickly discovered when they nosed around that fine old neighborhood."

"He couldn't possibly have done it, could he?" In the few times she'd been around him, Catherine had developed a genuine fondness for Charlie, although the tone of her question carried a ring of uncertainty.

"Of course not! I told you what he said today about Edwina's going to Horvath's bar all the time. I think the secret to what happened may lie there."

"But wouldn't the police have already checked out that possibility?"

"They might have visited the place, darling, but I

hardly think they'd spend much time there. Why should they? After all, they believe they've already got their man. And I'm sure they're going to try to link him to the killings of the Degnan girl and those two women. They're absolutely desperate to get that case wrapped up and sent to trial."

She shuddered. "That's horrible, Steve."

"Yes it is. McCafferty's prime concern will not be who killed Edwina. His job is only to try to get Charlie off the hook, and he'll have to do that by attacking the State's Attorney's case."

"You don't sound very confident."

"There's not a lot to be confident about. As good a defense attorney as this silver-tongued Irishman is supposed to be, he simply may not be good enough this time around."

Catherine began clearing the table. "Have you got a better idea?"

I think she knew what was coming–in fact, I'm sure she did. "I'm going to do a little looking around at Horvath's," I said in what I hoped was a matter-of-fact tone.

She sat down, crossed her arms, and fixed me with those wonderful, penetrating gray eyes. "Steve, I won't try to talk you out of it, but are you really sure this is a good idea? You know how you seem to attract trouble. There was that night down in Beverly Hills that you told me about years later, and that rough business at the University of Chicago during the war, when that guy tried to strangle you. You were lucky both times. How many lives do you think you've got left?"

"At least as many as a cat," I answered. "Hey, it'll be all right. I'm not going to take any foolish chances."

"Promise me that you'll be careful–extra careful," Catherine said. "You never know what kind of people hang out in these bars."

"And some of them are people who are a lot like me," I said with a rueful smile. I was referring to the uncounted hours I had spent in 'Killer' Kilkenny's saloon up on North Clark Street in the years between my marriages, when drinking was more important to me than anything else, including my work. "I will be home early, that I promise."

CHAPTER 7

I drove east to Pilsen for the second time in the last few days. I had passed Horvath's Tap many times on visits back to the old neighborhood to see my folks, but had never set foot inside. Turns out I hadn't missed much.

The corner tavern fronted on 18th Street, occupying the first floor of a three-story brick walkup, with what I assumed were apartments on the upper floors. The wooden sign over the door proclaiming its name was hand-lettered and faded, the paint peeling.

The small horizontal window next to the door was filled with a red-and-blue neon Pabst Blue Ribbon emblem. Inside, the joint was dark and stale-smelling, a beery, all-too-familiar saloon odor.

A half dozen men and a couple of women sat at the bar, which must have been about forty feet long, and a few couples were scattered through the booths. The jukebox was playing "To Each His Own" by Eddie Howard as I dropped onto a stool near the left end, three seats from the nearest other patron.

"What'll it be?" the tall, bony bartender muttered listlessly.

"A Schlitz on draught and a minute of your time."

"The Schlitz you can have," he grunted, walking along the bar to the pull. He drew a glass of the beer with just the right amount of foam and shuffled back, banging it down in front of me. "That'll be four bits, or do you want to run a tab?"

I dropped two quarters on the worn and nicked mahogany surface. "I've got some questions," I told him.

"Well, I ain't got any answers," he sneered. "In case you didn't notice, I'm at work."

I leaned forward on my stool. "Yeah, and really exerting yourself, by the way. How'd you like to keep working, Mac," I mouthed quietly, but in the most belligerent tone I could muster.

"What the hell's that supposed to mean? You pickin' a fight with me, *Mac*?"

"Not if you drop that surly attitude of yours and listen for a minute."

He put his hands on his hips and considered me through heavy-lidded eyes. "You a cop?"

"Nope. I'm a newspaper reporter–*Tribune*–working out of Police Headquarters." I flashed my press card. "I've got some questions about Edwina Malek, the woman who was killed last–"

"That didn't have nothin' at all to do with this place," the bartender growled. "Cops have already been in here asking questions, and I don't need to waste my time talking to any damned reporters."

"Oh, I think you do," I said, still keeping my voice low enough not to be heard over the music. "You own this fine establishment?"

"Part owner," he huffed, sticking out his long, thin jaw. "What's it to you?"

"I may not be a cop, but I've got lots of friends on the force. More important where you're concerned, I've also got friends–some very important, very powerful friends in…the…Building…Department. Got it?"

He opened his mouth to speak, but I made a slicing motion with my hand to cut him off. "They owe me some favors, if you get my drift. I wonder if your wiring is up to code," I said, looking around. "They've been getting a lot tougher on that sort of thing, as you may be aware. What about your plumbing? An inspector been around lately?"

"Few months back," he mumbled, running his rag absently over the surface of the bar.

"Seems like they're probably due to come back real soon, huh? You should know that there's a really tough new inspector on the plumbing side. Talk is that he's closed down two bars in Austin and another one up Lakeview way until they fix their problems. Nailed the doors closed.

"I can get you the names of the places if you're interested. Be a shame to have this joint shuttered. Looks like a nice spot for neighborhood folks to gather. But, well, the law's the law, right? And there's also a mean bird who does the electrical inspections now…"

The barkeep—I soon learned that his name was Maury—made a face and let out air. "Okay, okay, what is it that you're after?"

"Names. Names of people in here who'd been friendly with Edwina. And, by the way, nobody else who hangs around this place needs to know that I'm with a newspaper, got it? If I find out you've told anybody, you can be damned sure some city inspectors will start showing up real soon. Now, what about some names?"

"I gave the cop who came in here a few, but he didn't seem to care," Maury said. "He was just going all around the neighborhood talking to people. After all, it was the husband what did it, right?"

"Maybe. But I happen to be the curious sort," I said, pulling out my reporter's notebook. "Let's start."

He wasn't happy, but that was hardly my concern. "Well, first off, there's a woman, but I haven't seen her tonight," he said, scanning the room. "She's a regular, nice lady named Marge. She and Edwina were pretty chummy."

"Her last name?"

"Don't know for sure that I've ever even heard it," Maury said, stepping away to fill a drink order at the other end of the bar.

"Does this Marge come in here most nights?" I asked when he returned.

"Pretty much. She's a war widow. I think her husband caught it in the D-Day invasion."

"Attractive?"

He nodded. "And lively, too, at least sometimes, when she's not thinkin' about her dead husband. She and Edwina liked to sit at the bar. Marge and the guys were always after Edwina to sing. She had a real good voice, said she wanted to be a nightclub singer some day. I'd rather listen to her than most of this stuff on the jukebox," he added, jerking a thumb in the direction of the brightly lit music machine in the corner.

"So she could really liven the place up, huh?"

"Oh, yeah. And the two women, they both laughed a lot, but I think Marge, she forced herself to be cheerful sometimes. Anyway, the guys enjoyed hanging around them."

"Is that all that the guys enjoyed?"

"Look, Mister, I don't go snoopin' around into the lives of my customers. That ain't my way. I figure a tavern is a place where people are entitled to their personal privacy. Lot of 'em come in here to get away from their troubles."

"I totally agree about the privacy thing, except that this happens to be a murder case, and murder is hardly a private issue. Who were these guys that liked to hang around the ladies?"

"You didn't get any of their names from me, see?" he said, leaning toward me. "I don't want no trouble."

"Okay. It's a deal. Go ahead."

"Well, there's Karl, last name's Bohemian, begins

with a 'V.' Something like Vocek." He spelled it.

"A regular?"

"Pretty much, although he hasn't been in tonight, either. Not yet, anyway." Maury left again to serve another beer to a loud guy down the bar who was telling Negro and Jewish jokes. "So there's this rabbi, see, and—"

Mercifully, I didn't hear the rest of the joke because a new song on the jukebox drowned out the loudmouth.

"Any idea where this Karl lives?" I asked when Maury came back.

"Someplace close by. I think he walks here."

"What does he do?"

"Works as a foreman at that big Western Electric plant out in Cicero."

"Making telephones, eh?"

Maury nodded. "I guess. That's what they do there. I never asked him."

"He married?"

"No business of mine."

"That's not an answer to the question."

He gritted his teeth. "Yeah, he's got a wife. Never met her, though."

"What's he like?"

"Tough customer. Seems to be grumbling about something whenever he comes in. His job, or his wife, or the White Sox, or the weather. It's always something, that's just the way he is. I think Edwina and Marge both saw him as a challenge. They teased him a lot to loosen him up, and he got so he liked it. They actually got him laughing quite a bit, and he loved to hear Edwina sing, particularly that one from the war, 'A Nightingale Sang in Berkeley Square.' He musta asked for it almost every time she came in."

"And she'd always sing it?"

"Hell, yes. She loved being asked. She sang quite a bit in here. Said she wanted to do it professionally some day. Just like some English singer, name was Vera Lynn, I think. I never heard of her."

"Your loss," I said scribbling some notes. "Who else liked Edwina?"

Maury looked uncomfortable. He clearly wasn't enjoying the conversation. "Len, last name of Rollins. And before you ask, he lives in the neighborhood, smokes like a chimney, is single, and works on the loading dock of a furniture warehouse over on Loomis down near the canals."

"Hey, you're getting very good at anticipating my questions, Maury. Rollins a regular in here?"

"Yeah, pretty much. He's down at the other end of the bar now," the barkeep said, lowering his voice unnecessarily, given the noise level in the room. "He's the short guy in the brown jacket, wearing a flat cap."

"Oh yeah, I see him," I said after I'd leaned back and peered around the backs of several others hunched on their stools. Rollins, who looked to be short, was puffing on a cigarette and looking straight ahead with glazed eyes.

"What's he like?"

"Solemn sort, hits the bottle pretty hard, but don't quote me on that," Maury answered. "Hard to get more than a sentence at a time out of him. Funny thing, though: He's another one what loosened up around Edwina. She could really bring those guys out of their shells. She was good for this place, too," he added in a melancholy tone.

"Now she could be kinda sarcastic when you first met her, but once she got to know you, she was very friendly. Loved to joke, too. She had a sort of English sense of humor that really got the boys going."

"Didn't care much for her husband, though, did she?"

"Never met him," Maury huffed.

"She talk much about him?"

"Enough so you knew she wasn't very happy at home, I'll say that much."

"What was her beef?"

"Said all he ever did was work, day and night. Weekends. Never gave her any money, never wanted to go out anywhere. Guy sounds like he's a real stick-in-the-mud as well as a goddamn murderer. But I guess you think somebody else did it, huh?" he spat, daring me to contradict him.

"Maybe. I just like to be sure."

"Why're you so interested, anyway? What do you know that the coppers don't know?"

"I happen to know Edwina's husband, and he's just about the last person in the world capable of committing murder," I said quietly.

"So you're conducting your own investigation, huh? Cops ain't hardly gonna like that," Maury said without hostility.

"Like I told you before, they know me. We get along. So that's two guys so far who liked to spend time around Edwina when she dropped in here. Anybody else?"

He wrinkled up his face and stroked his oversized chin. "*Mmm*, well, there's Johnny Sulski, of course, and Big Ben Barnstable."

"Barnstable? The old light heavyweight, right?"

"Yep, that's him. Doesn't box any more these days, of course. Says he took his share of punches over the years, and that was more than enough."

"I seem to recall that he gave as good as he got, though. What's he doing now?"

"Works in some gym out around Madison and Central. Even helps manage the place, far as I know, and works with the young fighters."

"What's he like?"

A shrug. "Easygoing. You might think that he'd be one rough customer, given his old line of work, but he's as gentle as a lamb, always in good humor. Loved to spend time around Edwina. She asked him all about prize fighting and was fascinated by his stories of life in the ring and all those characters he fought. Sometime back in the thirties, they say he went six rounds with Braddock once, and was still on his feet at the end–this against a heavyweight, no less, and a one-time champ to boot."

"He married?"

"Divorced, far as I know. Comes in here three, maybe four times a week. He's not here now, though."

"And that other joe you mentioned?"

Maury went away to pour another drink, this one for Rollins, and came back to the quieter end of the room. "Johnny Sulski? He was here earlier, just for one beer. Said he had to be someplace else."

"And he's a regular?"

"'Bout as much as anybody. He's here most nights."

"And he liked Edwina?"

"A lot, I would say. He's the most tight-lipped one of the bunch, even more than Rollins down there," he said, motioning his head toward the other end of the bar. "But like with the others, that Edwina, she had a way of amusing Johnny. She could make him laugh, loosen him up."

"What's Sulski's story?"

Maury clearly was uncomfortable with the grilling I was giving him, but he took a deep breath and went on. "Really can't tell you much about him at all. Couldn't even say if he's married, but if I was to guess, I'd say no. I know he does some kind of construction work, but that's about all I can tell you. Like I said, he pretty much keeps to himself."

"And you really don't know this Marge's last name?"

He wrinkled up his already lined face again, which

didn't flatter him. "I know she said one time awhile ago that, after her husband got killed, she took back her maiden name. It was another one of those there Czech names, or maybe Polish—begins with a 'B.'" He gave a sudden start and nodded toward the door. "There she is now. Why don't you ask her yourself?"

CHAPTER 8

The woman who walked in seemed almost to be in a trance. I wouldn't have called her beautiful in any sort of traditional way, but she had an ineffable dignity. I pegged her age at about twenty-six. She was somewhere between a brunette and a redhead–her shoulder-length hair was parted in the center, framing an oval face and almond-shaped blue eyes that recently had shed tears.

The men hunkered along the bar rotated in unison on their stools, several greeting her in subdued, respectful tones. The room grew quiet, the tune on the jukebox having just ended.

"Hey, Marge, terrible about Edwina, wasn't it?" one said. Another mumbled something similar. She nodded to them, biting her lower lip, and headed for an empty seat near me at the bar.

"Hello, Maury," she said to the bartender in a throaty voice barely above a whisper. "Can I have a bourbon highball, please?"

"For you, it's on the house, Marge."

I turned toward her as she eased onto a stool. "No, I'd like it to be on me," I told the bartender. "Give me a

Schlitz on draught while you're at it."

"I don't believe I know you," she responded without emotion.

"You don't, but I'd like to change that. My name is Steve Malek. Edwina was my cousin's wife."

"Really?" She raised her eyebrows, her face finally showing a hint of animation. "I'm Marge, Marge Blazek. Charlie, he's your cousin?"

I nodded as Maury set the drinks in front of us.

"How...how is he?"

"Charlie? About like you'd expect under the circumstances–depressed, scared, in mourning, the whole works."

She moved over to the stool next to mine, fixing me with those light blue eyes that didn't seem to go with her chestnut hair. I had to admit, however, that the overall effect was by no means displeasing.

"He just could not have done it. Never," she said with quiet conviction, balling up small fists and pounding them on her knees.

"You know him well?" I asked, lighting the cigarette she had pulled from her purse.

She shrugged. "Enough to know that he wouldn't have killed her."

"But they were having some problems, right?" I asked, of course knowing the answer but wanting to hear her thoughts.

"Well...yes, so I heard. But after all, so do lots of

couples."

"Edwina ever talk to you about her marriage and her home life?"

Marge sucked on her lower lip and took a sip of the highball. "Sometimes. She got awfully lonesome in the apartment because Charlie worked so much overtime. He usually didn't get home before 9:00 or 10:00, she said."

"Uh-huh. And I understand she was pretty popular with a number of the men who hang out in the bar."

"Well, there are some guys in here who...enjoyed her company. You have to understand, she was very lively, very animated, and she could be really funny, too. An English sense of humor, I guess. Strange that you should turn up. I was going to talk to the police tomorrow."

"Really? About what? Or who?"

She looked around the room furtively and lowered her voice, even though with the music playing on the jukebox again, I could barely hear her from two feet away. "Somehow, I feel like I can trust you."

"Try me."

She dipped her head, as if that would make her voice even harder to overhear.

"Ever since...ever since what happened, I've been trying to remember everything from in here."

"Meaning what?"

"All the things that were said between Edwina and the guys at the bar. And all the things that were said about her when she wasn't here. I don't think I got even an hour's sleep last night."

"What did you come up with?"

She finished her drink and sighed. "Four of them who came in here a lot were especially interested in her, and I think at least two had been with her away from Horvath's, although I wouldn't ever swear to that. She didn't talk much to me about that part of her life. It was as if she didn't want anybody—even me, maybe her closest friend around here—to know that she was...well, she was seeing people, people besides Charlie."

I figured that the four names were the same ones Maury had reluctantly coughed up, but I wanted to hear them from Marge Blazek's very own cerise lips. "So, who are they?" I prodded.

She looked around again, as if surrounded by people leaning in with ears cupped, hanging on her every word. "There's Sulski, of course. Johnny Sulski."

"Why do you say 'of course'? What's the dope on him?"

"Well, it seems like he's always around, except he's not here tonight. He was pretty sweet on Eddie. Always tried to make sure he sat next to her at the bar. Always whispering things to her, and then she would blush or laugh, or both."

"Did it bother him that she was married?"

Marge eyed a cobweb on the ceiling, then turned back to face me. "Guy like Johnny, you could never tell what he was thinking. Doesn't say much most of the time. Kind of a loner. I been coming in here longer than Eddie, and before she started showing up, I hardly ever knew Johnny to talk to anybody. He would just sit at one end of the bar nursing beers and not saying a word, like he didn't want company or conversation or anything like that.

"I think Eddie saw him as a challenge," Marge went on. "She teased him and started asking him stuff about himself."

"And she finally got him loosened up, is that it?"

"Right. Pretty soon, it got so that when he came in, usually around 5:30 or so, he'd make sure nobody sat at the stool next to him. That was reserved for Eddie."

"Does this Sulski have a wife?"

"Funny thing is, I don't know for sure. I don't even know exactly what kind of work he does. I think maybe he's a plasterer or a stonemason, and if Eddie knew, she never told me."

"Were the two of them having a fling?"

"I'd guess not, but I honestly don't know. For all that Eddie and I joked around here in the bar, we really didn't discuss our personal lives hardly at all. We didn't really see each other except in here."

I ordered her another highball and lit up a Lucky. "What about your own personal life, Marge?" I asked with a smile, trying to keep the question casual.

"Not much to say about it these days," she answered somberly, contemplating the new drink. "I was married, but my husband, Dave was his name, got killed in the D-

Day invasion. We were only married for a few months. Since then...oh, I come in here and joke with the guys a lot, have a few drinks and all, but I don't go out much. On dates, I mean."

"I'm sorry to hear about Dave," I told her, meaning it. "What do you do when you're not in here?"

"I work in a women's dress shop a few blocks west along 18th Street. And I live in the same apartment I grew up in right near there. My parents are both gone now."

"Mine too, and I grew up just a few blocks from here, too, although I've lived elsewhere for a long time. Back to Edwina. What about the others who come in here and who showed some interest in her?"

"Well, there's Len Rollins, he's down there at the end of the bar, wearing a flat cap, leaning on his elbows," she said, still in a lower-than-necessary voice. "About as quiet as Johnny but, like with Johnny, Eddie got him to loosen up and laugh. She could really bring people out of their shell."

"I'll ask the same question as with Sulski: Do you think they had something going outside of this place?"

"I dunno. S'pose anything's possible," she murmured with a shrug, looking toward Rollins as if he might somehow be able to hear her over the din.

"Tell you what," I said, "why don't we take our drinks over to a table, where there's a little more privacy."

Marge nodded, and we walked across the creaky wooden floor to one of the booths. Two or three of the stool denizens turned to take note, then swiveled back to their drinks.

"This'll give 'em something to talk about," she chuckled. "You're married, right?" Her eyes were on the band on my left-hand ring finger.

"Right. For the record, my wife knows I'm here."

"Hey, sorry, I didn't mean to be nosy. No offense meant."

"None taken. So, we've got Johnny Sulski and Len Rollins showing some degree of interest in Edwina. The others?"

"Well, there's Karl–I don't know his last name. Comes in often, but he's not here now."

"Tell me about him."

"Oh, he's really not a bad guy, although he puts on this grumpy act, see. At least I think it's an act. He's always complaining about something. The weather's too cold, or too rainy, or not rainy enough, or he's mad at his boss over at Western Electric, or his neighbor's dog is barking at night. You might call him a Gloomy Gus."

"Married?"

"That's another thing! He's always mad about something that he says his wife did, the poor woman. She can't possibly be as bad as he says."

"You know her?"

"Oh, no. It's just that it sounds like she has to put up with a lot from Karl."

"The guy doesn't sound like he's easy to like. What

was the situation with him and Edwina?"

"He could walk in here crabbing about Lord knows what, and within five minutes Eddie would have him laughing and grinning and even buying a round for everyone in the place. It was amazing the effect that she had on him."

"So, here's the same question as with the others. Were–"

Marge smiled for the first time since walking in. "I know, I know, were they having an affair?" The smile faded. "It's a possibility, I guess. Hell, the way Karl would look at Eddie like a lovesick puppy, and the way he would glare at Johnny Sulski, who was always trying to keep her to himself. I always thought the two of them might start slugging it out over her sometime, but they never did."

"That leaves one other name."

She nodded. "Yeah, and that's the one guy who could really have done some slugging if he'd wanted to, although he's a very gentle type. Former boxer named Ben Barnstable."

"I remember him. Even saw him fight once, years ago."

"Sure, lots of people did, so I've been told, although I don't know anything at all about boxing. Meeting him, it's hard to believe he ever pounded on people with his fists. Probably the most good-natured regular this joint has."

"But he's not here tonight?"

"No. You'd know right away if he was around.

Booming voice, laughs a lot. Loves to tell stories about his days as a fighter. He works with young boxers someplace in town now, helping 'em develop. And I'll beat you to the punch. Get it–the *punch*? Like in boxing? Anyway, before you ask, I can't tell you for sure what, if anything, was going on between Ben and Eddie. I do know that he liked her a lot–that was easy for anyone to see. And she loved to hear the stories about his fighting career. She would ask him all sorts of questions just to keep him spinning yarns. You could tell it got both Karl and Johnny riled up."

"Is Barnstable married?"

"Divorced. The only reason I know is that he mentioned it once or twice. The way Ben told stories, it didn't take long to learn pretty much his whole life history, but he wasn't boring about it. Not at all. He wasn't a bragger, because he told a lot of stories on himself, actually made fun of himself. He really, truly, has had a colorful life, far more interesting than anybody else's background in here."

"But you wouldn't want to guess if anything was going on between him and Edwina?"

She ground out her cigarette in the metal Pabst Blue Ribbon ashtray. "Well, this much I *can* say. Another woman who drops by here occasionally, name's Doris, came in late one night awhile back and mentioned to me that she'd seen Ben and Eddie walking on the other side of the street from here, a few blocks south of 18th. They were under a streetlight, and they were arm in arm. But that doesn't really mean all that much, does it?"

"Maybe, maybe not. I'm interested in something you said right after we started talking."

She cocked her head. "Yeah?"

"Something about your wanting to go to the police. What for?"

"I just know that somebody other than Charlie must have killed her."

"You got a better candidate?"

She took a deep breath, then another. "It had to be somebody from in here."

I lit another cigarette for her. "You've got my full attention."

"These guys, the four we talked about–every one was absolutely crazy over her."

"Hardly a reason for murder. Men have been crazy over dames ever since that poor schnook Samson let one of them cut off his hair and rob him of his strength."

"Yeah, but I think that each of these four was truly enchanted by Eddie. And they all heard her complain enough about Charlie that they felt she was looking for...well, I guess you could call it some sort of *comforting*. And, as I think you can tell from what I've been saying, she could be something of a flirt."

"So I'm beginning to learn. I only saw her cranky, nagging side when she and Charlie had dinner at our place a couple of times. So, what did you plan to tell the police?"

She sampled her second drink, which gave her time to choose her words. "I wasn't exactly sure, except to mention that those four all seemed almost bewitched by her. I heard that they, the cops, had been in here asking questions, but they were just going through the motions, according to Maury. He said they didn't seem too interested in this joint or any of the people who hang out here."

"Maury's right," I told her. "They figured they already had their man. They really were just going through the motions. Probably some neighbor of Charlie and Edwina told the cops she hung out in here. While we're on the subject of these four men, is there one above the others that you'd finger as the killer if you had to make a choice?"

More sipping of her drink. "It's hard to believe somebody you know might be a...murderer," she murmured.

"Yeah, but just a minute ago, you said you thought it had to be one of them. You can't have it both ways. You got a favorite?"

"Well, yes." She looked around again for those nonexistent eavesdroppers. Everybody sitting at the bar had their backs to us. "I think it's Johnny Sulski."

"Interesting. Any particular reason?"

"Well, of all of them, he was the most jealous and the most...I guess you'd say...intense. And he has a temper. I saw an example of it in here once, long before Eddie started hanging out. Some fellow I'd never seen came in, sat at the bar, and made some half-joking comment to Maury about how lazy construction workers are. Johnny blew his stack, called the guy all kinds of names–some of which I'd never even heard before–and invited him outside into the alley."

"Did they end up slugging it out?"

She shook her head. "Un-uh. The new guy, he wasn't about to fight. He just told Sulski he didn't mean anything by what he said, and walked out. Far as I know, he's never been back."

"Probably the smartest thing he could have done, from the way you describe Sulski. So, if it was really Sulski who killed her, what do you think happened with him and Edwina that night?" I asked as I lit another cigarette for Marge.

"I'd be guessing."

"Go ahead and guess. There's absolutely no charge for it."

"I think Johnny went over to her flat–hers and Charlie's–and made some moves toward her. She resisted and somehow she ended up getting stabbed. Maybe she got the knife from someplace, probably the kitchen, and was trying to use it to protect herself from Johnny and they wrestled with it. It was probably an accident."

"If it really was Sulski, the guy took quite a chance by showing up at the apartment. He and Charlie probably came within just minutes of running into each other."

"Really?" she said, startled. "I thought Eddie was killed early in the evening, and Charlie always works late."

"You're right, that's usually the case, but that night there was no overtime. That's also why he's in the soup now; he's got no alibi. There's nobody to say he was anyplace except in their apartment. If he had worked overtime, he would have had his fellow workers to vouch for him."

She put a hand to her mouth in shock. "I really gotta talk to the police and tell them what I think happened," she gasped.

"Let me handle this," I said, holding up a hand." I've got some connections."

Her eyes widened. "You a cop?" she asked breathlessly.

"Let's just say that I spend a lot of time around cops and leave it at that."

"Are you some kind of private detective?"

"Sort of, I guess. I'm a police reporter for the *Tribune*. But I'd appreciate it if you kept that to yourself."

She was still wide-eyed. "I will. What are you going to do?"

"First off, I'd like to talk to the four guys you told me about. Not tonight—only one of them is here anyway—but over the next several days. One at a time, of course."

"But shouldn't something be done right now?"

"There's really not all that much of a hurry, Marge. In

the first place, the so-called wheels of justice tend to turn very slowly, even in a murder case. Charlie's going to be cooling his heels in the Bridewell for some time. Also, we've hired one of the best defense lawyers in the city for him, a guy named Liam McCafferty, so nothing figures to happen right away."

She looked doubtful. "So then you don't think I should say anything to the cops?"

"To be honest, even if you did, it wouldn't help right now. But here's something you can do: Next time I'm in here, you can point out those guys to me. Now I already know who Rollins over there is," I said, nodding toward the bar. "So I'll need you to finger Sulski, Barnstable, and Karl, whose last name we don't know."

"Geez, how am I going to do that without them thinking something funny's going on? Wouldn't it look weird, me pointing a finger at one of them for you?"

"I think we can figure out a way to be a little more subtle about it," I replied in what I hoped was a reassuring tone.

"But when will you be back?"

"Well, tomorrow's Saturday, and I've been told by my wife that we've got plans for the evening. This place is open Sundays, right?"

"Yeah, and it's usually pretty crowded."

"It's a deal. Let me give you my phone numbers at work and at home," I said, pulling out my notebook. I scribbled them on a sheet, tore it out, and handed it to her.

"Why don't you give me any numbers where I can reach you?"

She gave me her home number and the one at the store, both of which I wrote down.

"How about 7:30 Sunday night?" I asked.

"I'll be here," Marge said, sounding as though she'd rather not.

CHAPTER 9

After I finally had worn Catherine down and she agreed to marry me, we talked for a long time about where we would live. I was in favor of somewhere on the north side of Chicago, mainly because it was familiar to me. I had lived in Logan Square with Norma during the last several years of our marriage, and then I had a three-room apartment on North Clark Street near Wrigley Field, as a bachelor for eight years after the divorce.

However, I realized almost from the first that Catherine wanted to be wedded not just to me, but also to Oak Park, where she had lived all of her life, except for the two years of her own unfortunate marriage, when she resided right next door in Berwyn. She specifically wanted to stay in the solid old stucco house on Scoville Avenue where she had grown up and then returned to for the last dozen years or more, taking care of her increasingly senile father, the once-great police reporter Lemuel 'Steel Trap' Bascomb.

After Steel Trap died in '42, she stayed put in the roomy, two-story house with the elm-shaded yard. The truth was, she wanted to live there more than I wanted to live anywhere else, so I yielded. Besides, I'd come to rather like the village myself. It seemed to be a graceful combination of half-city, half-suburb. But our understanding from the beginning was that I would bear the lion's share of the expenses. Something to do with pride—no pun intended.

Another reason Catherine was wedded to Oak Park was the job that she loved—assistant librarian at the village's public library, where she had worked for close to a dozen years.

So it was that I moved into the stucco on Scoville. As it turned out, I also went to Catherine's church, although not every Sunday. I was willing to change for the lady, but only up to a point. She was a regular attendee at a place of worship on Lake Street, a few blocks from the house, called Unity Temple, which was part of a denomination I'd never heard of—Universalist.

It was about as far from my own religious experience as I could imagine. Although long since lapsed, I had been raised Catholic and grew up attending mass in an ornate Pilsen sanctuary filled with incense and candles, statues, and white-skirted altar boys, and the Latin liturgy, of course. This Oak Park church, if you can call it that, is a square, mostly windowless, concrete building that is widely recognized as an architectural landmark.

Services take place in a two-story-high room, also square, with seats rising steeply on all sides and with a surprising amount of natural light streaming in through a gridwork of twenty-five skylights recessed into the coffered ceiling.

The worship itself was, to me at least, surprisingly informal, with a homily–sermon, rather–that could just as easily be about politics or education as about religious themes. Having said that, I found the whole experience to be somehow refreshing. I can only imagine what my late, sainted mother would have thought of that spiritual journey.

I bring this up because Unity Temple would arise the next morning in conversation.

When I got back home from Horvath's Friday night, Catherine first expressed relief that I was home safely, then pressed me for details about the evening. I filled her in on Maury and Marge and the four men they had named as particular 'friends' of Edwina's.

"So you're going back to that bar and talk to all four of them?" Catherine asked, concern evident in her tone. "Is that wise? Why not tell the police and let them do the questioning?"

"As I said before, they think they've got their man. They've already been to the bar, and they're not about to send detectives out again on what they view as a fool's errand."

"That really puts Charlie in a bad–oh, wait a minute, Steve. I almost forgot! That lawyer you got for him, McCafferty, called tonight. He needs to talk to you. I told him you'd be home late, and he said that he'd be in his office tomorrow, even though it's Saturday. He said for you to call him there."

First thing the next morning, I phoned Liam McCafferty, who picked up on the first ring. "Ah, yes, Mr. Malek. I thought you should know that your cousin is not being overly cooperative."

"Oh? How so?"

"I cannot be specific, of course–attorney-client privilege and all–but Mr. Charles Malek does not seem to be interested in helping himself. Indeed, he does not seem the least bit concerned about his fate."

"In your experience, is that unusual in situations like this?"

"Very much so. Even though the loss of a loved one can be devastating, in almost all cases a defendant places self-preservation above all else. Your cousin does not at the moment seem overly interested in self-preservation, however. May I impose upon you to intercede with him?"

"Yes, of course. I'll try to see him later today or tomorrow. How would you describe his mental state?"

"Depressed. Extremely depressed and fatalistic about his future."

I told McCafferty that I would call him with a report after seeing Charlie, then joined Catherine at the kitchen table for breakfast.

"Steve, do you remember that I asked you to keep

tonight open?"

"Yes, right, although to be honest, I'd almost forgotten. Is there a movie you want to see over at the Lake or the Lamar?"

"No, it's to do with Unity Temple. You may recall my telling you that it was designed by the famous architect Frank Lloyd Wright. Well, they're marking the fortieth anniversary of the building's construction tonight, and Mr. Wright is coming to give a lecture about it."

"Hmm. I think I'll pass on that. I'm not sure I want to...wait a minute! I've just changed my mind in mid-sentence. Yes, by all means, let's go. I want to meet this Frank Lloyd Wright fellow. He and I might just be able to do some business."

Catherine gave me a puzzled look, but before she could respond, our back doorbell rang. It was old Mrs. Anderson, the widow who lived next door. She was returning a casserole dish she had borrowed.

"Oh, come on in, Mrs. A.," Catherine said cheerfully, "and have a cup of coffee."

"Well...all right, but I'll only stay for a few minutes. I don't want to interrupt your morning."

"You're not interrupting anything. We've just finished breakfast, and are having another cup ourselves, right, Steve?"

"Right. Have a seat, Mrs. A. It's always nice to see you."

Mrs. Anderson rarely smiled, and she did not make an

exception this morning although she did toss off a nod in my direction, which for her was an animated response.

"I'm glad you stopped by," Catherine said as she poured coffee for our visitor. "We're going to the Unity Temple tonight to hear Frank Lloyd Wright speak, and I thought you might like to come along with us."

The elderly woman reacted with what I would describe as a fierce frown. "Huh! I would not walk across the street to hear that devil," she snorted. "Don't you know about him? He used to live here in Oak Park, way back when—but of course you're both far too young to remember that. He designed all sorts of houses, had a big family and all—six kids. Was very well known and well paid, a real big shot.

"Then do you know what he did? Left his wife and children, that's what. Just went off to Europe or someplace in about '08 or '09 with another woman from right here in the village, the wife of a client, yet! Named Cheney. They both up and deserted their families, just like that. It was the biggest scandal this town's ever seen. It was talked about for years afterwards.

"A few years later, the Cheney woman he ran away with—well, I say that what happened then was God's own avenging hand at work. She and some others got burned to death in a fire at Wright's place in Wisconsin that was set by some crazed servant. The big shot himself should have died, too, but he was someplace else at the time. Lord knows he deserved to die—a sinner of the very highest order. No, thank you anyway, my dear," she said, putting a hand on Catherine's arm. "I shall not be going to hear the great Mr. Frank Lloyd Wright!"

Before going to listen to this "sinner of the very highest order," I made my second trip of the week to the Bridewell. I was parked in a visitors' chair when Charlie shuffled over and slumped down on the other side of the screen. He had been fairly low when I'd visited him before, but now he was even lower. If I were to liken his expression to that of a dog, the breed would be a basset.

"Hello, Stevie," he said in a voice devoid of emotion.

"Hi, Charlie. I understand that you've met Liam McCafferty."

"Yeah. He was in here yesterday."

"He told me you didn't seem interested in what might happen to you."

"What's the point, Stevie?" he sighed. "They're determined to strap me into that chair."

"Nonsense! You've got the best damn lawyer in the city. He's got a terrific record, and I'm zeroing in on some possible suspects. I spent last night at Horvath's."

He just shook his head. "Nothing's going to matter, Stevie."

"Goddamn it, don't talk that way! Now listen to me: I want you to cooperate with McCafferty...tell him anything you can think of, no matter how unimportant it seems to you, that might help your situation. We're going to get you out of this mess, but you've got to help yourself."

He nodded without conviction, staring down at his hands on the metal surface of the counter.

"All right, McCafferty will be back here to see you, probably on Monday, and you will help him to help you. Do you hear me?"

"Okay, Stevie," he said, but I had a feeling that my pep talk had fallen flat.

CHAPTER 10

The sanctuary in Unity Temple was close to full when Catherine and I arrived a few minutes before 7:30. Our aged neighbor may not have forgiven the architect his transgressions, but apparently many others in the community had—or else they either weren't aware of those transgressions or didn't gave a rap.

A tall, very slender, silver-haired woman in a tailored blue suit stepped to the rostrum and favored us with a broad smile. "My, but it's nice to see so many of you here tonight on this very special occasion in the life of our temple. I won't ask for a show of hands to see who among you remembers when this wonderful building was completed, but I will confess that I was here myself at the time. Of course, I was very, very young then," she said with a self-deprecating chuckle.

She waited for the requisite tittering to die down before continuing. "We are so privileged tonight to have the world-renowned architect himself here to talk to us about this masterpiece of design. It gives me great pleasure to present...Mr. Frank...Lloyd...Wright!"

The great man suddenly materialized. Apparently, he

had been behind a door, waiting like one of the Barrymores to pop out and make a dramatic entrance onstage. And he got applause worthy of a Barrymore.

Although in his late seventies and brandishing a cane, Wright was still an imposing figure in a black cape, a long crimson scarf, and his trademark wide-brimmed, flat-crowned hat. At a quick glance, he could have passed for a Roman Catholic bishop.

He doffed the hat, flipping it casually aside in what probably was a practiced motion, then stepped to the rostrum–or was it a pulpit?–surveying his audience with piercing eyes.

"Here," he intoned, spreading his arms wide, palms up, and looking up as if embracing the heavens, "is the very place where modern architecture was born. Look around you, all. This is a hallowed place. Is it any wonder that people travel here from the world over just to see this edifice, this temple, this welcome haven of refuge in the midst of that hurly-burly existence we call urban living?"

He was just getting warmed up. He ran a hand through his thinning white hair and leaned on the lectern.

"My goal here was not merely to create a religious structure, but one that fully embodies the principles of liberal religion for which this church stands: unity, truth, beauty, simplicity, freedom, and reason. Here is where you will find the first real expression of the idea that space within the building is the *reality* of the building. And it glows with the same radiance today as when it first opened its doors to its worshipers almost four decades ago. I remember that time as if it were yesterday."

The architect went on to discuss his storied career, focusing on such seminal structures as Tokyo's Imperial Hotel; the Johnson's Wax headquarters in Racine, Wis.; Fallingwater, the dramatic house built over a waterfall in rural Pennsylvania; and the Guggenheim art museum in New York City, which was still on the drawing boards.

Using no notes, he then talked in general about architecture and his other favorite subject–himself. I scribbled down a few of his better quotes: "The mother art is architecture." "Without an architecture of our own, we have no soul of our own civilization." "Every great architect is, necessarily, a great poet. He must be a great original interpreter of his time, his day, his age." "My *lieber meister,* Louis Sullivan, once said that 'form follows function.' That quote has, I believe, been misunderstood. Form and function should be one," he said, interlacing the fingers of his hands, "joined in a spiritual union."

Then, in self-revelation, he added: "Early in life, I had to choose between honest arrogance and hypocritical humility. I chose the former and see no reason to change."

After tossing off a few more aphorisms, he glanced at his watch: "I see that I have exceeded my allotted time. I thank you very much for your attention." As he bowed theatrically and stepped back from the lectern to enthusiastic applause, the blue-suited lady came forward.

"Thank you so much," she said to the architect. "What

a simply grand evening, and it's not over yet! Mr. Wright has graciously agreed to take questions from the audience, and immediately afterward we will be serving coffee and sweets in Unity House, which adjoins this sanctuary."

Hands flew up around the room, and the Mrs. Blue Suit pointed to one. "Mr. Wright," asked a bald man toward the back, "what is your favorite design creation?"

"The one that's on my drawing board at that moment," he answered to laughter.

"Mr. Wright, what do you think of Mies van der Rohe?" posed a woman down in front who wore a large, broad-brimmed hat with flowers on it.

"A truly engaging fellow. Likes good cigars and fine wine. I must say that I enjoy his company. But what he needs is to spend some time with me and my boys up at Taliesin learning about organic architecture. It would do him a world of good. He has been quoted as saying 'less is more.' Sometimes with Mr. Mies, less really is less." That drew a few laughs and a smug smile from Wright.

"How do you feel about Eero Saarinen's work?" came a question from the upper level.

"I traveled to South America with his father once, and all I learned from him was how to fill out an expense account. (*more laughter*) I've never met this younger Saarinen, but based on his work, I would term him possibly the best of the eclectic architects," he said dismissively.

After Wright had aimed a few more barbs at other

architects and their work while heaping praise on himself, our mistress of ceremonies called a halt to the festivities, and we all migrated over to the social hall. Catherine and I stood at the outer edge of a throng that pressed in on Wright, asking questions and seeking autographs. Some had copies of his books that they asked him to sign. He smiled beatifically and patiently responded to each query and request, perhaps hoping there might be a prospective client somewhere in this well-to-do suburban assemblage.

Gradually, the crowd dispersed in the direction of the refreshments, and I approached the man himself.

"Mr. Wright, my name is Steve Malek. I'm a reporter with the *Chicago Tribune.*"

"Mr. Malek," he acknowledged with a nod, indicating that because of a cup of coffee in one hand and a cane in the other, he was unable to shake hands. "Do you know what I've said about journalists?"

"I'm afraid I don't."

His eyes twinkled. "I'm all in favor of keeping dangerous weapons out of the hands of fools. Let's start with typewriters."

"Interesting words," I parried, "from someone who has used the press so skillfully over the years."

"Well said! Well said!" Wright responded with a hearty laugh. "How did you like my talk?"

"Entertaining, I must say. I have a proposition for you."

"Indeed?" He raised his eyebrows.

"My son is an architecture student at the University of Illinois in Champaign, and–"

"I am so sorry to hear that," Wright snapped.

"Yes, I know a little about your attitude toward architectural schools."

"Which is why I created our own school, up at Taliesin."

"That's precisely what I want to talk to you about. I'd like you to take my son on this summer, as an intern there."

"Mr...Malek, is it? We do *not* engage summer interns at Taliesin," Wright harrumphed.

"Oh, I am sorry to hear that. I was hoping that we might come to an accommodation."

He arched his brows again. "Oh? What sort of an accommodation?"

"As I said, I'm a reporter with the *Tribune,* which, as you probably are aware, has one of the largest circulations of any newspaper in the U.S."

"Your point being?"

"My point being that I think it's time for a major Sunday feature on you and your work in the *Tribune*. A feature that I would write. Over the years, you have shown tremendous resiliency, and today your popularity is greater than ever."

"Don't patronize me, Mr. Malek."

"Far be it for me to do that, Mr. Wright," I shot back. "I'm merely stating a fact. People want to know what you are doing today, and what your thoughts are on the current state of American architecture. We all got some insight on the latter tonight, I might add, at the risk of being accused, once again, of patronizing you."

Wright's eyes narrowed to slits. "A Sunday feature in the *Tribune*, you say?"

"Yes."

"What makes you qualified to write such a feature?"

"One, I am an excellent writer, or perhaps 'superb' is a more apt adjective. Two, I am an extremely skilled interviewer. Three, I study my subject and his work thoroughly before any interview." I thought I'd throw my own self-confidence right back at this supremely confident egotist.

"Would this feature have photographs of the...subject, and of his work?"

"Of course. Probably in rotogravure color."

"And I take it that you are suggesting a quid pro quo involving your son?"

"Precisely."

The architect pursed his lips. "I don't believe that I can do that," he said, thumping his cane twice on the floor to underscore his words.

"A pity. Chicago readers would have loved to get an update on your work and your theories about design and the future of architecture."

"I will not be blackmailed," he said, but his tone began to lack conviction.

"Of course not. You are well known for sticking to your principles, and I respect you for it. If you don't want to do the interview, I'll have to go to my fall-back position with the *Tribune's* editors."

"And what would that be?"

"A Sunday feature on your friend Ludwig Mies van der Rohe. Now that he's building what amounts to a whole new campus for the Illinois Institute of Technology on the south side of Chicago, he'll be of particular interest to our readers. As you yourself said a few minutes ago, he's an engaging fellow. I'm sure he would make a fascinating subject."

"Do your editors know that you operate this way?" Wright snapped.

"What way is that? I just know that they're looking for a feature on architecture right now," I lied. "I'm sure they would be equally happy with an article on you or on Mies."

"There's no comparison!" he barked, thumping his cane on the floor several times and causing several people to throw puzzled looks in our direction.

"You were my first choice," I conceded. "And I thought you might be pleased that I think enough of your work to suggest my son could benefit from a summer of study under your tutelage at Taliesin."

"Of course he could benefit from it! God knows what notions they're filling his head with at that mass-production design factory down there in Champaign. All right, Mr. Malek," Wright said grudgingly. "I believe we can find a spot for your son this summer up in our verdant hills of Wisconsin." We exchanged phone numbers and agreed to work toward finding a time for the interview on Wright's next trip to Chicago.

I thanked him and went to rejoin Catherine, who had watched our conversation with a puzzled expression. I was a bit puzzled myself as to how to proceed. Mike Kennedy, the *Trib*'s Sunday Editor, had liked the magazine-length features I had done for him in the past, many of them built around interviews. The question now was whether he would find an architect who was pushing eighty a compelling enough figure to be the subject of a major article.

CHAPTER 11

On Sunday night I drove back to Horvath's, pulling into a parking place across the street at precisely seven-thirty. Marge Blazek, raincoat collar pulled up tight around her neck against the April gusts, was standing under a street light a few doors away.

"Over here," she called as I stepped out of the coupe. "I thought it would be better if we weren't seen in there together again."

"It doesn't bother me any," I said, "but it's your hangout, so it's really your decision. Without you, though, how am I going to identify these guys, other than Rollins, whom you've already pointed out?"

"I've been in the bar already, checking it out for you. The only one there now is Ben Barnstable, who's hard to miss. He's wearing a brown leather jacket and Levi's, and he's sitting at the far left end of the bar. I stopped in to have a drink a little while ago and told everybody that I'd probably return a little later. If I do come back, I'll give you a casual 'hello,' that's all."

"I don't mean to drive you away from your favorite hangout just because I'm muddling around in there," I told her.

"No, no, it's okay. I probably spend too much time in the joint anyway. Besides, I don't want that gang to think I'm some sort of a snitch."

"I get you. All right, maybe I'll see you later tonight, maybe I won't," I said over my shoulder as I headed across the street to Horvath's.

The room was fairly crowded and even smokier than on my earlier visit. Barnstable was indeed hard to miss, even from behind. He was nearly half a head taller than anyone else sitting at the bar, and a quick glance told me he must be at least twenty or thirty pounds heavier than in his days as a light heavyweight. I sauntered over to an open, stool-less spot at his left and nodded my greetings to the bartender. "Evening, Maury. I'll have a Schlitz on draught."

He eyed me warily but said nothing, then drew the beer and placed it on a limp coaster in front of me.

"Windy night, huh?" I said to Barnstable, who was nursing a highball.

"Sure is, mate. Like to blow me right over, big as I am."

"Name's Steve Malek," I told him, holding out a paw.

"Howdy. Ben Barnstable," he drawled, shaking hands with a strong grip.

I tried to look surprised. "Really? Hey, that would be 'Big Ben' Barnstable?"

"That's me all right," he said, his square-jawed,

freckled face lighting up with a lopsided 'aw-shucks' grin worthy of Jimmy Stewart. He must have been a pretty good boxer, because his face was essentially unmarked—no cauliflower ears like so many former boxers sport, one thin scar above his left eyebrow, and a nose that had been slightly displaced to the right.

"Hey, this is really something. I was in the crowd up at the Marigold Gardens back in '39, I think it was, when you went ten rounds with Kid McCoy. That was one helluva bout. You knocked him down four times, if I remember right."

"You sure do remember right," he nodded, the grin even wider. "What you might not recall is that he knocked me down three times, himself. That boy could punch. He had a left that could rearrange your face."

"I knew that he'd decked you. But you won on a split decision, if I remember it right, didn't you?"

"Darn right. The referee, Tommy Carstairs it was, gave me the edge by a pretty good margin. The two judges each had it closer, but one of 'em gave me the nod. That was prob'ly the best fight of my career.

"That and the time I went six rounds against Jimmy Braddock, although I took a pounding in that one. I was lucky the Mick didn't knock me out. He had me on the ropes in the fourth and again in the fifth, although I gave him somethin' to remember in the sixth, a right cross that made his eyes roll right up outta sight. Thought I had him knocked out then, but damn, he was tough. His knees buckled when I gave him that right, but the Mick never went down."

"Back to your fight with McCoy. He even had a shot at the light-heavy crown once, didn't he?"

"Right you are...Malek, isn't it? He got knocked out by Gus Lesnevich in a title bout a few years ago now. 'Course, that's no disgrace. Gus has knocked out lots of people. I wouldn'ta wanted to face him, although I never got the chance."

"I used to walk to the Marigold up there at Grace and Halsted when I lived on Clark Street. I was there when the young Joe Louis KOed Buck Everett back in '34 or so. I also saw Johnny Bratton and Lee Savold knock people around in that ring."

"Darn, those are great names, and the Marigold's a great place," Barnstable agreed. "I still go up there to watch the bouts. Had my first Chicago fight there, after coming up here from Tennessee. God that seems like a long time ago. Hey, you really know your boxing, don'tcha?" he said approvingly.

I shrugged and lit a Lucky. "Guess I got hooked after watching that big Dempsey-Tunney fight at Soldier Field back in the Twenties."

"Damn, how I wished I'd seen that one," Barnstable said in an awed tone. "Most famous fight ever. I was still back in Memphis then, fighting in little clubs for ten- and twenty-buck purses. I got twenty-five for a bout once and thought I was the luckiest guy in the whole state."

"You could probably write a book about your boxing career," I observed.

He laughed heartily. "Shoot, I can hardly even write at all, other than my name. But I been lucky. I seen me a lot of interesting places, all 'cause of the boxing. Been to Pittsburgh, Buffalo, Miami, Los Angeles, Detroit—even fought on the under card at the Garden in New York once, before a welterweight title bout in '35 where Barney Ross beat Jimmy McLarnin. I won my bout that night, then went up into the stands, and watched the main event. I 'specially remember it because Jack Dempsey himself was the referee. How 'bout that, huh? Dempsey himself."

"Great stories. What're you doing nowadays, Ben?"

Barnstable leaned a meaty arm on the bar. "I help out in a gym up on Madison near Central. Work a lot with the young guys comin' up—get 'em into shape for the Golden Gloves matches or maybe to help start their pro careers. There's a lotta good young boxers around this town. One of our local boys just knocked out the fifth-ranked lightweight in Cleveland last week. He's got a great future."

"Sounds like you're doing what you like to do."

He nodded. "Yeah, I do love bein' around that gym. The workouts, the punching bag, the three-rounders. Kenny Waters, the guy what owns the place, pays me a decent wage. Shoot, I ain't really fit for much other kinds of work."

"Well, you're helping your own sport, and I'd say

that's pretty important. Say, Ben, can I talk to you about something else?"

"Sure, I guess. What's on your mind?"

"Edwina Malek."

His open, guileless face darkened. "Eddie. Oh, Eddie. Terrible."

"Yes, it was. She was married to my cousin Charlie."

Barnstable jerked upright and turned to me, squinting. "The guy what killed her?"

"That has yet to be proven," I replied.

"From what I been hearing, the cops think it was him," he stated.

"That's what I understand, but I don't believe it, and not just because he's my cousin. He's the farthest thing from violent."

The former boxer contemplated his drink. "She was a great gal," he said in a husky voice. "I liked her...I liked her a real lot."

"I understand she was very popular with everybody in here. Can I buy you a drink?"

He nodded, expressionless. I signaled Maury and pointed to the nearly empty highball glass. After the new drink was delivered, I suggested to Barnstable that we go to a booth and talk about Edwina. He didn't seem enthused by the idea, but he got up silently and followed me to the other side of the room.

"I didn't really know her all that well," I told him when we were seated. "My wife and I had them over to our place in Oak Park for dinner a couple of times, and that was really it. I'd like to learn more about what she was like."

Barnstable looked like he was going to start crying, but he controlled himself. "I think maybe...maybe I loved her," he muttered.

"You two spend much time together?"

He blushed. "That's the funny part. We never had us what you'd call a real date or anything like that. Just about everything was in here." He made a sweeping gesture, encompassing the room. "A lot of the time, it wasn't just Eddie and me talking. It was a whole bunch of us with her."

"What made her so special to you?"

He ran a thick hand through his mop of dense black hair flecked with gray. "She made me feel like I was special. Always asking me about my life and my boxing and everything. I was married once, and my wife was never like that, never. She married me 'cause it looked like I was goin' places back in them days. She figured she'd be the wife of a champ sometime, but then when things didn't go so well for me in the ring, she was gone. Just up and left one day. Eddie, now, she was different."

"She was also married."

Barnstable nodded glumly. "Yeah."

"Did she talk much about her husband?"

He screwed up his face. "Hey, I don't wanna go and say bad things about your cousin."

"It wouldn't be *you* saying them, Ben. They would be Edwina's words. Besides, I have at least some idea of what their relationship was like."

He still looked uncomfortable. "Well, I do know she was mad because he was always workin', always overtime, every night it seemed. She wanted to go places, like movies, dancing, restaurants, stuff like that. She was full of life, full of fun, and she loved to sing."

"Did you ever hear her talk about getting a divorce?"

"Uh, sorta. She said life over here–in the U.S., I mean–wasn't quite how she thought it was gonna be."

"Meaning it was not as much fun?"

"Partly, I think. From what she told me a few times, it seemed like she had thought maybe she was gonna be living a lot better than she really was, you know?"

"Yeah. I think that a lot of the war brides feel just the same way, Ben. When you're away from this country, like I was for awhile right at the end of the war, you realize that a lot of people in Europe believe that we're all millionaires, all living the kinds of lives they associate with royalty."

Barnstable chewed on his lower lip. "It was funny. Sometimes she'd be teasing, joking, telling all sorts of funny stories about England, getting everybody in here to laugh and even sing songs along with her, like that 'Berkeley Square.' Other times, she'd walk in all sad and blue, not wanting to hardly talk to anyone at all."

"Sounds like she might have been manic-depressive."

"I wouldn't know nothin' about that, but it seemed like she could be two different people sometimes."

"But you liked her a lot anyway?"

He nodded vigorously. "Heck, yes. I woulda done just about anything for Eddie. If she hadn't been married, I'd have asked her to go out with me, on a real date. Maybe to the movies or a restaurant. I woulda been proud to be seen with her."

"For the sake of argument, let's say that my cousin Charlie was not her killer. Who do you think might have done it?"

He sat for a half-minute, resting his chin on his hands. "I just wouldn't know that. Not at all. Sorry."

"You indicated she was very popular in here. I assume that means several of the guys who hang around Horvath's liked her, right?"

"Uh-huh. It was sort of a competition as to who would sit next to her at the bar."

"Did you usually win that competition?"

"No, not always."

"You could have pushed everybody else aside."

"Nah. I'm not like that. Since I quit the ring, and that's, let's see…'bout seven, eight years ago, I've never been in a fight, never used my fists. And I'm never gonna."

"That speaks well for you, Ben. Who else liked to sit with Edwina?"

He laughed dryly. "Better question is, who didn't?

Johnny Sulski usually beat everybody else to it. Made sure he got here early, and he saved Eddie a stool right next to him."

"Didn't that piss you—and the other guys—off?"

"Me, I'm pretty easygoing, like I said before. But I think Len Rollins and Karl Voyczek, they got pretty hot sometimes about the way Johnny was trying to keep her to himself."

"Both of them liked Edwina a lot, too?"

"Oh, yeah, sure. They was sweet on her. Of course, so was Johnny."

"What about one of those three as the murder candidate, Ben?"

He shook his head vigorously. "Nah, they all liked her too much to ever hurt her."

"Let's say one of them went to her apartment and tried to make a pass at her. Let's also say she didn't like that. She could have gotten a knife from a kitchen drawer and then wrestled around with him, whoever it was, and the knife went into her chest—an accident, of course. What do you think, Ben?"

"I don't think none of these guys woulda made a pass at her like that," Barnstable said, but he sounded uncertain.

"Anybody else who came in here show a lot of interest in Edwina?"

"Oh, maybe a few. She was easy to like, at least when she was in a playful mood. But I'd say it was mainly the four of us who we've been talking about."

"How 'bout anybody else who might have wandered in? Somebody who wasn't a regular?"

"I seen that a few times, and Eddie usually wasn't so friendly with them as she was with us. In fact...there was some guy who came in here a few weeks back, I remember now. He tried to make time with her, but she threw cold water on him. Not really, but you know what I mean. She did let him buy her a drink, though. I was a couple of stools away and could hear them.

"She started complaining about her husband—your cousin—and how he was never around, always at work. And just before the guy left, she said she'd like to 'kill the bloody bastard.' I remember them words exactly." He shook his head and looked down.

"Did she mean the guy at the bar?"

"No, not him!" Barnstable said as though I were dense. "She meant her husband. After she was killed, I remember thinking maybe he killed her because he was afraid she was gonna kill *him*. 'Cept that I can't hardly imagine Eddie ever killin' nobody."

"Hmm, interesting. Ben, think back to last Wednesday night, around 6:30 or 7:00, which was when Edwina was stabbed. Were any of those three—Sulski, Rollins, Voyczek—in here at the time?" I purposely avoided asking Barnstable about himself, at least for the moment, figuring it might come out in the conversation. It did.

"I couldn't tell you that, 'cause I wasn't here myself until later in the evening."

"Probably working late at the gym, eh?"

"No, I been puttin' on weight these last few years," he said, patting his outsized stomach, "so I been doin' a lot of fast walking after work, several miles maybe two, maybe three times a week. Wednesday was one of them nights."

"I would have thought that you'd get plenty of exercise at the gym."

"Yeah, you'd think so," he said, seemingly unaware that he was being questioned, "but in there I spend all my time working with the young boxers, so I'm not doin' anything to take care of this." He rubbed his tummy again. "Say, here I been talkin' away all about myself. I'm good at that." He laughed at himself. "I never even asked what you do."

"I do some investigating."

His face registered modest surprise. "Really? You mean like a cop?"

"Sort of," I said. "In this situation, though, it's a family thing rather than work."

"Well, I wish I coulda helped you, and I sure hope for your sake it ain't your cousin what done it. But if he did, he'll have to pay, of course."

I nodded and said goodbye, heading for the door. My plan was to return the next night and meet one or more of Edwina's other 'friends.' But plans have a way of getting altered.

CHAPTER 12

When I got to my desk in the Headquarters press room at nine on Monday morning, I was hoping that nobody would ask me about Charlie's situation. I didn't like being personally involved in a news story, even in the somewhat peripheral role of cousin to a murder suspect. Besides, there was nothing new to report at the moment anyway.

I needn't have been concerned, however. This being the first week of the new season, it was only natural that baseball was the prime topic of discussion.

"Hey, I've got a great idea for a pool," Packy Farmer rasped between puffs on one of his grotesque little hand-rolled smokes. "We all throw in five bucks and write down where in the standings we think the Cubs are going to finish. In October, the one who's closest wins the fins."

"And just what happens if more than one of us picks 'em in the same spot, Einstein?" Dirk O'Farrell asked.

"Very simple, my good man," Farmer answered, tapping the side of his head. "Given my superior brain-power, I have anticipated your query. There's a tiebreaker, see? Everybody writes down the number of victories they think our Wrigley boys are going to get. The one who picks them in the right spot *and* is closest in the win column goes home with the dough. Nothin' to it."

"Wonder if anybody will pick them to finish first?" O'Farrell asked.

"Doubtful, Dirk," Anson Masters proclaimed. "Sure, they won the pennant last year alright, but none of their starting lineup had to go off to war. Cavarretta, Pafko, Nicholson, Lowery, Merullo, Passeau, Borowy...they were either 4-F or too old to get drafted. Other teams had some of their best players in the service, and those boys, like Musial of the Cardinals and Williams of the Red Sox, among others, will be back playing this year."

"As much as it pains me to say so, you're right, Anson," I put in. "Hell, the Cubs would have won the World Series last fall if the Tigers hadn't got that guy Virgil Trucks back from the war just in time to pitch in the Series and win one game. As it was, our boys took the Tigers all the way to seven games before losing. Without Trucks back with them, we probably would have won the whole thing.

"But there are a lot more like Musial and Williams and Trucks and DiMaggio coming back from the service to play this year. Our boys will be fielding pretty much the same squad as last year. No improvement."

"Yeah, there's no possible way the Cubs can win it all," Eddie Metz of the *Times* agreed. Eddie never had an original thought...he usually waited until somebody took a position and then agreed with it.

"Well, are you all in or not?" Farmer demanded.

"Sure, why not," O'Farrell said, taking a five dollar bill from his pocket and waving it. "In for a penny, in for a pound, as they say. But I want an impartial observer to hold the dough and the predictions. I vote for Nick here, our City News friend. On his salary, we won't push him to join the pool, but he can be the keeper of the ballots and the greenbacks."

"Fine by me," Nick said. "Do you want me to put them in a locked drawer?"

"Damn right," I said. "Who knows if one of these miscreants here might take to peeking at the others' picks along about September and alter his own selection?"

"And that includes the well-known rascal Snap Malek of Colonel R.R. McCormick's *Tribune*," O'Farrell said. I thumbed my nose at Dirk and wrote down my prediction, handing it to Nick along with five singles. (For the record, I would end up winning the pool in October, picking the Cubs correctly for third place, and beating Eddie Metz in the tiebreaker by coming within one of the number of victories they recorded.)

After the balloting was concluded, we all dispersed to our beats around the building, which meant I walked down the usual one flight and presented myself to Elsie Dugo Cascio, guardian of the gate to Chief Fergus Fahey's office.

"My goodness, is it that time already?" she said,

looking at her wristwatch. "How the minutes do fly by around here."

"Only when you're really having fun," I replied. "I trust that his eminence is on the premises this fine morning?"

"He is indeed. I will announce your arrival." She mouthed my name into the intercom and he made a groaning sound, which meant he was girding for my invasion.

"Morning, Fergus. Nice to see you in such fine fettle, whatever that means," I said, sitting and flipping a half-full pack of Luckies onto his blotter. "Have a good weekend?"

He looked up from a stack of paperwork and said something that sounded like "Grmmph."

"I'll take that to mean yes. Anything going on that Chicago's newspaper readers are simply dying to know today?"

"Far as I'm concerned, not a damn thing," he snarled, pulling a cigarette out of my pack and lighting up.

"Which means, of course, that there's nothing new on the Degnan case?"

"Correct."

"What about Edwina Malek's murder?"

"What about it?"

"Are your boys doing any further digging?"

Fahey leaned back and closed his eyes long enough that he might silently have been counting to ten. "Snap, as far as I'm concerned, there's no earthly reason that they should be."

"Meaning, of course, that it's a foregone conclusion that my cousin is a murderer."

Fahey turned a hand over. "After all, he has been arraigned."

"There happened to be a batch of guys hanging around a saloon who were interested in Edwina Malek, who was known to frequent the very saloon herself. Any one of them could have done it."

"And how, if I may be so bold as to ask, do you happen to know this?"

I knew he wasn't going to like my answer. "I've been spending time in said saloon in Pilsen where she used to hang out."

"Goddamn it, Snap! Haven't you got yourself in enough trouble over the years by playing amateur copper? You're lucky to be alive."

"Charlie didn't do it, Fergus, and somebody has to find out who did. Looks like that's going to have to be me."

"Not that you're likely to take my advice, but your best bet right now is to go out and hire a good lawyer for your cousin."

"I already have–Liam McCafferty. See, Fergus, sometimes I really do take your advice."

"McCafferty, eh?" He whistled. "That's gonna be costly. Your cousin have that kind of dough?"

"He's getting some help," I said.

"Hmm. Now I wonder who from? Well, you can't do much better than the glib Irishman. Shit, with him on the job, I'd say your boy's chances are starting to look pretty good."

"But not good enough for me," I shot back. "For one thing, even the great McCafferty loses cases, albeit on rare occasions. For another, even if he were to get Charlie off, there would always be the suspicion that he really was the killer, and that the only reason he was walking around free was that he had a brilliant mouthpiece on his side. I plan to nail the murderer, with or without the help of Chicago's finest, and it looks like it's going to be without."

Fahey scowled. "I suppose it does no good to tell you to be careful."

"Why, Fergus," I said with a tight smile, "you know that I always listen to you."

He muttered something unintelligible and returned to his never-ending paperwork as I got up and left.

Back in the pressroom, I dialed McCafferty's office. This time, the ever-so-cool woman who answers the phone was actually borderline pleasant and put me right through when I gave her my name. Ah, the joys of being a client.

"How did your second talk with my cousin go?" I asked him.

"A marginal improvement," he answered dryly. "I must say, though, that the lad still doesn't seem overly interested in his own future."

"I'm sorry to hear that. Well, while you're working on his defense, I'm trying to find out who else might have done the killing."

"Just how might you be going about that?" he asked warily.

"There's this bar down in Pilsen where Edwina spent a lot of evenings, as Charlie may or may not have told you. Turns out she drew quite a crowd of would-be swains around her there. It seems there was what might be termed a spirited competition for the lady's affections."

"That so?"

"Indeed. And I'm in the process of getting to know some of these Lotharios."

"Well, I have a few freelance investigators of my own that I find occasion to utilize from time to time. Would they be of any help to you in this endeavor?"

"Right now, I think I'll keep pushing on myself. Thanks anyway, though."

"Well, be careful," the lawyer cautioned. "Saloons often draw an unsavory lot, as I'm sure you are aware."

"You're the second person who's urged caution to me in the last ten minutes, and I assure you that I appreciate the advice. We'll talk soon."

The rest of the morning was uneventful. I had a sandwich with Packy Farmer at a little café a block from headquarters and got back to my desk a few minutes after one. I was about to call Marge Blazek at her dress shop and set up a plan for that night in the hopes of meeting another of the men who found Edwina beguiling. I had just begun to dial when Anson Masters of the *Daily News* picked up his own ringing phone.

"What? My God," he barked into the mouthpiece with what for him was uncharacteristic emotion. "When? Jesus, that's terrible! Just awful!"

Everyone had turned toward the pillar of the pressroom. "Well, it's outside the department's jurisdiction, but of course I'll check to see if they're sending any technicians or medical people out to the site. Yes, I'll get back to you right away."

He cradled the phone, and took a deep breath. "My city desk. There has been a disastrous railway crash far out in the western suburbs, in Naperville. Two streamlined Burlington passenger trains. One rammed the other, apparently at a high speed. Tore it all to pieces. Bodies all over the place along the tracks. The desk says it looks like one of the worst train wrecks on record."

Before any of the others in the room could react, my phone rang. It was Hal Murray, the *Trib's* day city editor. "Malek, there's been a railroad smashup out in Naperville—a real big one. Lots of fatals."

"I know. I just heard the word."

"Listen, we're really short-handed here," he barked in his typical machine gun-style cadence. "I got three guys down with that damned flu that's going around now, and a couple of others are at a three-alarm fire in a plant out on the northwest side that's getting bigger. I need you out in Naperville to do the feature stuff. Eyewitnesses, human interest, that kinda thing, you know. Unless you've got something really hot going on there."

"No, I don't."

"Good. We've already sent Phillips to do the Page One piece, although he's probably not out there yet. You can grab a ride with Cappelitti. He's just heading out the door to his car now. I'll catch him and have him pick you up in front of Headquarters."

"I'll be waiting for him."

CHAPTER 13

Lido Cappelitti was one of the best photographers on the *Trib* staff–maybe *the* best. He was damned good company as well, as I learned from the few times I'd worked with him over the years.

His battered green Dodge with its dented right front fender and cracked rear window never fully came to a stop in front of Police Headquarters. I jumped onto the running board and swung inside as we tore away to the screeching of tires.

"How you doin', Snap? It's been awhile," he jawed out of the corner of his mouth, as he lighted a Chesterfield, and steered with his knees. Lido couldn't have been more than five feet six, but when he was on the scene of a story, he had the voice and presence of a burly six-footer. You could hear him a half block away, bellowing orders, telling people how he wanted them posed, or hectoring a cop to "give me some space to take my shot here, will ya, Sarge?"

He wheeled the whining Dodge through the streets of the near south side, ignoring traffic lights and leaning on his horn with the confidence and panache of a driver who had a newspaper press photographer's card clearly visible on the inside of the windshield. Soon we hit Ogden Avenue, which would take us all the way out to Naperville, located in the farmlands some 30 miles west.

We finally cleared the Chicago city limits and raced through what seemed like an endless string of suburbs: Cicero... Berwyn... Lyons... Brookfield... LaGrange... Western Springs... Hinsdale... Downers Grove. Once we finally got to Naperville, Lido seemed to know where the wreck site was.

"I been in this burg before," he told me through clenched teeth that held the fifth Chesterfield of the drive. "Didn't ever expect to be covering a story like this here, though."

Never having set foot in the town, I was glad he knew his way around. We turned south off of Ogden into a residential street and soon found ourselves at a police barricade. "Road closed from here to the tracks," a uniformed local cop told Lido.

"We're with the *Tribune*. We need to get through right away," the photographer told him brusquely, gesturing to the press card on the windshield. "We're on deadline, and every second counts!" But, it was obvious that a mention of the newspaper and its immediate needs did not carry the same weight out here as it did in the city.

"Sorry, sir, but this is as far as the car goes," the cop responded, calm and unimpressed. "You'll have to walk the last block or so. Won't kill ya."

Lido scowled and swore under his breath, but we were left with no option. Sirens blared from all directions, and cops, firemen, and just plain civilians were running in every direction. I stuck my press card in my hatband and, as we were getting out of the car, a silver-haired woman in a housedress and bedroom slippers ran by us crying, "It's awful, awful! Somebody do something! For God's sake, do something!" I tried to stop her, but she pushed me away like a football player stiff-arming a tackler and kept on running, yelling, and waving her pudgy arms, her slippers going "flap, flap, flap" on the pavement as she ran.

I followed the squat, camera-toting photographer, stepping over fire hoses and weaving through the increasingly dense crowd of onlookers. When we came within sight of the tracks, we both put on the brakes.

It was a scene I never hope to view the likes of again. What I soon learned was that the last passenger car of the lead westbound train, the Advance Flyer, had been cleaved in half by the second train, the Exposition Flyer, whose silver diesel locomotive was embedded deep into the wreckage, with dust and smoke still rising from the destroyed coach.

Groans and screams came from the shattered car even now, some two hours after the crash. Bodies, some of them children, were sprawled along the tracks.

Firemen and other rescuers picked their way through the shambles, hauling passengers–many of them corpses–

out through the windows of the train car or through the gaping holes where the sides of the car used to be.

Crews used acetylene torches, cutting away the metal to reach those who were trapped. The survivors, many of them blood-spattered and maimed, were being trundled on stretchers over to waiting ambulances. Lido was right there with his camera, snapping pictures and barking at rescuers to stop blocking his shots.

I spotted our general assignment reporter, Dean Phillips, talking to a fireman, and I joined him. "Any idea how many fatalities, Chief?" Phillips asked, notebook in hand, as he nodded his recognition to me.

"Too soon to tell yet," the grim-faced firefighter replied, wiping his grimy brow. "I know they've taken out at least twenty bodies so far, and there are lots more in there. Right now, we're mainly trying to get the rest of the living out of that hellhole. Some of them are pinned in pretty badly, as you can hear. I gotta go," he said, turning away and heading toward the trains.

"Snap, glad to see you here," Phillips said. "You're doing the sidebar stuff, right?"

"Yeah. I'll start looking for eyewitnesses."

"Good, you ought to find plenty of 'em. I'm off to talk to the cops and also somebody from the Chicago, Burlington & Quincy line to find out what the hell went haywire. See you later."

He went off as I watched members of the rescue crews moving into and around the passenger cars, which were strewn along the tracks at crazy angles like a kid's electric train that had derailed on a living room floor around the Christmas tree.

A group of students from nearby North Central College had arrived to help with the injured, as had employees from the big Kroehler furniture plant that overlooked the crash site. I interviewed one of the college kids, a red-haired twenty-year-old North Central sophomore, who had been a stretcher-bearer and was understandably teary and distraught about the agony he had witnessed. There was no shortage of help, but getting the injured through the crowds of onlookers at the scene and off to hospitals seemed to be the biggest challenge at the moment.

An elderly fellow in a flat cap and lightweight jacket sat with his head in his hands on the curb of a street that adjoined the crash scene, his black-and-white cocker spaniel at his side.

"Are you all right, sir?" I asked, crouching next to him. He looked up, dazed, shaking his head.

"Were you on the train?"

He shook his head, slack-jawed. "No, oh my, no. I live just a block from here. I was walking Bogart." He motioned toward the tail-wagging dog, which seemed unconcerned about the frenetic activity swirling around him. "We always take our walk at the same time every afternoon. I like to watch the trains come through, and so does Bogart. But today…"

"So you saw what happened then?"

"It was like watching the end of the world."

"I'm a reporter with the *Tribune*," I told him, gesturing to the press card in my hatband and pulling out my notebook. "Tell me what you saw."

He looked down at the pavement. "It was different today," he muttered. "For some reason, a train was stopped on the tracks, and these limiteds don't usually stop in Naperville. This is mainly a commuter train station. There musta been some sort of signal problem. Me and Bogart, we didn't think nothing of it. Then we could hear this other train a'coming. Sounded like it was moving awful fast, but there's three tracks here, and I figured it must have been on another track."

"But it wasn't."

Still looking down, he shook his head vigorously. "No, sir. It started blowing its horn, and then you could hear all this hissing and screeching...the brakes, I suppose. And then...it was like a sound I never heard before. A lot of sounds, really—a sort of squealing, this was probably the brakes and the wheels and all the steel smashing together, and then the breaking glass. I had to put my hands over my ears, and Bogart was barking and whining and all." He hugged himself and groaned at the memory.

"And you watched it?"

He let out perhaps the saddest sigh I've ever heard. "The engine, it just...it just ripped into the back end of the stalled train and tore it apart, like it was some kind of giant can opener. When the awful noise stopped, then… then it was even worse. You could hear all the screaming.

"Oh, my God, it was terrible. All those poor people." He started sobbing, and his faithful dog nuzzled his cheek with its nose.

I had scribbled down his narrative, and I got his name and age, which was seventy-eight. I could only hope that after this experience, he would make it to seventy-nine. As I walked away, he was still on the curb, sniffling and rocking, and cradling Bogart in his lap.

I walked on along the tracks to the west, passing cops barking orders, firemen and flashing lights, and ambulances. Farther from the point of impact, the cars of the front train didn't seem as badly damaged, but that may have been deceptive, given that when the crash occurred, passengers all through each of the two trains surely were thrown around like rag dolls and ended up bouncing off the walls, floors, and maybe even the ceilings.

I came upon a grandmotherly woman in a brown dress who was wringing her hands and crying softly. A small brown suitcase rested on the ground at her feet. "Are you hurt?" I asked, gently clasping her arm.

"Oh, no, no, thank you, I'm all right. Just shaken up," she said weakly, looking up at me through rimless glasses and trying without success to force a smile.

"You were on the train?"

"On the Advance Flyer, yes, sir. I was walking along

the aisle and got knocked down onto the floor, bumped my head, but it's not bad," she told me, indicating a small bruise on her forehead.

"I was one of the lucky ones, maybe because I was toward the front of the train. Although the woman in the seat in front of me, who was riding on to Denver, I'm afraid she might be... But right now, I'm very worried about my sister."

"You mean she's still in there?" I said excitedly, pointing to the train.

"Oh no, she's out in Omaha where we live, expecting me home tonight. But when she goes down to the station there to meet me, she'll find out about the wreck and will be terrified about what happened to me."

"Why don't you just telephone her?"

"Where would I do that?"

"Come with me," I said, taking her by the hand and leading her toward the red brick Naperville depot. Inside, three people were lined up to use the lone pay telephone in the waiting room. The woman at the phone was yelling into the mouthpiece that she was stranded. "Yes, yes, a crash—dead people all over the place! I'm in—what's this town?" she asked the man behind her in line, who told her. "I'm in a place called Naperville, somewhere west of Chicago. I'm in their station. What? Yes, I'll wait here...You'll drive? How long? Three hours?" She sighed. "Well, all right, if I have to, I just have to. I'll be right here then, on one of these hard wooden benches. Where else am I going to go? What choice do I have?"

The other calls were in a similar vein, including one from a woman who was asking a neighbor to check on her cat. "She'll be expecting me," the woman said of her pet. "She won't know what to think."

Finally, the little lady from Omaha had her turn at the instrument. "Oh, dear," she said, fishing in her purse. "I don't believe that I have enough quarters."

"Don't worry, I've got a pocket full of them," I assured her. She hooked up with the long-distance operator, and together we fed the requisite amount of silver into the slot. She reached her sister and filled her in on the situation.

"Well, I do feel better now," she said after hanging up. "Thank you so much for all of your help. Now I'll have to figure out where I'm going to stay tonight."

"I noticed a Red Cross truck just outside," I answered. "They probably can help you. I'm sure there must be some hotels nearby, maybe in Aurora, which is only a few miles west of here. The Red Cross people should be able to provide transportation for you. There are going to be a lot of folks in the same predicament as you, and with a little luck you can probably get a train to Omaha sometime tomorrow, assuming they get these tracks cleared."

I tried to press a few dollars on her, but she refused politely, thanking me again and giving me a hug. I went outside into the pandemonium to find more eyewitness accounts from other passengers and onlookers.

After I had gotten a few more quotes, I phoned the city desk from the depot's pay phone and dictated my piece to Williamson, one of our rewrite men. It ended up running on Page 3 along with the continuation of Phillips' headline story.

It was long after dark when Lido dropped me off at home. He'd already sent several rolls of film back to the office with a courier that the paper had hired. I had called Catherine to let her know where I was, and she held dinner for me.

"You got a call from a Marge Blazek," she said as we sat down at the table. "Said you should call her tomorrow at the store where she works. She's the one from that tavern that you mentioned, right?"

"Yep. As I told you before, she and Edwina apparently got pretty chummy from hanging out in Horvath's."

"But from what you said, it seems like it was Edwina who was getting all the attention from the men in there."

"True. Which is interesting, because I would say Marge is at least as attractive as Edwina, maybe more so."

"Really?" Catherine said, raising one eyebrow.

"Don't you go getting any ideas," I said, grinning and holding up a hand. "My interest is purely professional, or I guess I should say familial. It's with her help that I hope to get Cousin Charlie off the hook and out of the clink.

"As for why Marge didn't have the boys at Horvath's

falling all over her, I think it's because she's still mourning her husband's death, and it shows. She's got this aura of sadness about her, I guess you'd call it. Anyway, from what she told me, she's not ready to start dating anybody yet. It's been less than two years since D-Day."

"Uh-huh," Catherine said. "Back to Charlie. Has that hotshot LaSalle Street lawyer you got been any help?"

"McCafferty? Not so far, but then he's not getting a lot of cooperation from my dear cousin. It seems like Charlie has just given up and doesn't give a rap about what happens to him."

"He probably never was what you'd term a dynamo," Catherine observed. "I don't know him all that well, of course, but from what I've seen, he seems very passive, letting himself be swept along by circumstances rather than taking any kind of a positive stance in his life."

"True. He has always been that way, as long as I've known him. Probably goes back to that domineering mother of his. She ran the poor guy's life, as well as his father's."

"Well, he had darn well better get himself some gumption now," she said heatedly. "If he doesn't cooperate with that lawyer you hired, he'll likely be finished–*really* finished. From what you've said, it sounds like he still idealizes Edwina, despite the way she treated him."

"I'm not sure about that, but I've said a little myself to McCafferty about what she was like. Remember this: If Edwina gets painted in a really negative light, particularly as to how she treated Charlie, it will have the effect of fueling the state's case against him. As in, 'long-suffering husband finally reacts violently against wife who constantly nagged and carped at him.'"

Catherine nodded thoughtfully. "That's a good point, Steve. How bad do you think it is for Charlie?"

"Really, really bad. He has absolutely no alibi, other than 'I was on my way home from work.' There were no fingerprints on the knife, which means nothing in itself because whoever did the stabbing would have wiped it clean. And the only prints the cops found anywhere else in the apartment were Charlie's and Edwina's. So the only evidence is circumstantial, but that's the case in a lot of crimes where there's a guilty verdict."

"So you're left to find another candidate?"

"That's pretty much the situation, and I have to keep at it with these guys at Horvath's. They're the only hope, as far as I can see right now."

Catherine reached across the table and put a slender hand on my arm, squeezing it affectionately. "Please, please, be careful. You don't know what you're playing with here."

"You're right, but I'd hate myself if I didn't do everything I could to help Charlie. As we both are all too aware, he doesn't seem to be capable of helping himself."

CHAPTER 14

The first thing I did in the pressroom at Headquarters Tuesday morning was to call Marge Blazek at the dress shop.

"I thought I would hear from you yesterday," she said, sounding puzzled.

"You would have, except that I got called away to cover that train collision out in Naperville."

"Oh yes, they were talking about the wreck at Horvath's last night, and I heard more about it on the radio this morning. So many people killed."

"Yeah, it was truly dreadful. Like nothing I've ever seen before, or ever want to see again."

"Do you think that they suffered a lot–the ones who died?"

"Most of them probably didn't feel much, it all happened so quickly," I said, if only to make both of us feel better.

"Well, that's good anyway. Trains have always sort of scared me. Are you coming to Horvath's tonight?"

"Yes. You'll be there?"

"Like before, I'll wait across the street and let you

know which ones are inside."

"Is it really necessary to go through this elaborate charade?"

"These are...my friends. At least all but one of them is. And I don't want them to know I'm being–I don't know, disloyal, I suppose."

"But after all, to do otherwise would be disloyal to Edwina and her memory, wouldn't it?"

"Yes, but I just don't want to be in there when you're questioning these guys. Hey, I never asked you how it went with Ben Barnstable."

"Okay. He seems like a good guy, very open. You don't have to be with him very long to see that he had it bad for Edwina."

"I know. They all did, every one of them. And Ben is an especially nice guy."

We set seven-thirty once again as the time to meet. It was a few minutes before that when I pulled the coupe up to the curb across the street from Horvath's. Like before, Marge was waiting under the streetlight, her head wrapped in a blue babushka. I felt like I was an actor in a Grade B espionage film. All we needed was fog swirling around the streetlight and church bells tolling the hour.

"Aren't the folks in there getting suspicious of the way you come in for a little while and then duck out for the rest of the evening?" I asked.

"Not really. Like any bar, people are always coming and going. Nobody pays much attention to who's there and who isn't at any given time."

"Who's in there tonight?"

"Ben Barnstable again, but you've already talked to him. And Karl Voyczek."

"The one who works over at Western Electric and is always grumbling about something or other, right?"

"That's one way to describe him," she said with a tight smile. "He's there right now, sitting at the bar by himself as usual. He's husky, has dark hair cut short, and is wearing a black leather jacket. I talked to him a few minutes ago, and he was in his usual mood. Griping about the weather just as I left."

"Okay, I think I'll do some griping of my own," I said. I crossed the street and entered a joint that was becoming all too familiar to me. Two or three of the denizens turned as I walked in, and Ben Barnstable grinned, nodding his recognition. Voyczek was hunched over the bar, an empty stool on either side of him. Clearly, he was not the most popular joe in the place.

"Mind if I sit here, or are you saving it for someone?" I asked him.

He threw a scowl in my direction. "Like they say, it's a free country," he muttered. "Suit yourself."

"And a damned messed up country, too," I countered in my crabbiest tone, signaling Maury and ordering a Schlitz on tap. "Government's all screwed up. And they're treating the returning servicemen like dirt, if you ask me."

Voyczek shot me a brief glance but said nothing,

turning back to his own beer, Blue Ribbon from a bottle.

I went on. "Then there's Truman, who's supposed to be such a great friend of labor. Hah, that's a joke! If he's such a big buddy of the workingman, why are there so many strikes right now? Steel, meatpacking, the glass industry, and so forth. Everywhere you look. And the miners figure to be next, the way that bushy eyebrowed union boss of theirs, John L. Lewis, is acting. Why isn't the White House standing up for the unions and helping them get what they're asking?" I was on a roll.

"These are the same people who worked their fannies off in the plants and mills during the war so that our soldiers and sailors and marines could have what they needed to beat the Japs and the Krauts. And this is the thanks they get from their government.

"You know what our President said the other day? Claimed the big unions have too much power." (I neglected to mention that, in the same quote, Truman said that big business had too much power as well.) "Yeah, it's a messed up country right now," I snarled, taking a healthy swig of Schlitz and then lighting a Lucky.

"Damn right," Voyczek said, turning back toward me and nodding vigorously. He had a broad, high-cheeked Slavic face and squinty eyes with pupils that seemed as black as his hair. He looked more like a boxer than Ben Barnstable did. I put him at about forty, which would make him three years younger than me.

"You seem like somebody who knows what I'm

talking about," I said with an approving nod.

"I know what it's like to be screwed around with," he growled. "I was an assistant foreman for awhile, but the brass took that away from me, because I fought for the guys on the line. They didn't like that, the bastards."

"Where do you work?"

"Western Electric. Hawthorne Works. Cicero."

"That's one big plant."

"Yeah. Too damn big, if you ask me. You can get lost in the place, in more ways than one."

"Ever thought about going someplace else?"

Voyczek drank beer and stared at the liquor bottles lining the mirrored back bar. "Christ, I'd have to start over then. Besides, with all those veterans coming back now, the market is tight, really tight."

"Well, it could be worse. You could be one of those poor guys coming back from the war without a job—or a home. I read that there's thousands of them getting mustered out who have no place to live in this town. There's even been talk of hauling old streetcars out of the scrap yard and turning them into homes for the GIs. Imagine having to live in a rusty old red rattler. That's a real crime."

He shook his head. "Pathetic."

"I agree. I suppose I should introduce myself. Steve Malek."

"Karl Voyczek. Say, I never seen you around here before, have I?"

"I been in a few times, must have been nights you were someplace else. Maury, how about a couple more for us?" I yelled down the bar. If looks could kill, the bartender's glare would have struck me stone dead on the spot, but he managed to contain himself and placed our respective brands in front of us. "This one's on me," I said.

Voyczek started to object. "Hey, there's no need to do—"

I waved his objection aside. "Happy to buy one for a fellow workingman. You were as important to the war effort as our boys in Europe and the Pacific."

He clearly was not the talkative type, but my comment all but demanded a question from him. It came.

"What do you do for a living?" he asked.

"I'm sort of like an insurance investigator."

He nodded thoughtfully. "Which company?"

"Freelance."

"So you try to keep people from collecting what they're entitled to, huh?"

"Not really. I'd say that at least half the time, the policyholders get exactly what they asked for," I improvised.

He grunted, which I took to be agreement. It was time for me to shift gears.

"Did you know that murdered woman, the one that used to come in here?"

"Why are you askin'? Because of some life insurance policy on her?"

"No, not at all. My interest here is entirely different. So, you knew her?"

Voyczek took a deep breath, letting the air out slowly. "Yeah. I did."

"So did I. In fact, we were actually related. She was my first cousin's wife."

"That son of a bitch? No shit. Well, I guess he'll go to the chair now, huh?"

"That's assuming he did it," I said quietly.

"Who the hell else would'a done it?" he demanded as he stuck out his chin and turned to face me.

"Good question. That's exactly what I've been wondering for the last several days, because my cousin is the last guy in the world who would kill anyone. He's so passive he walks around ants on the sidewalk rather than step on them."

Voyczek seemed unimpressed. "It's those shy, quiet ones you gotta watch," he spat. "They keep stuff bottled up, and then they explode. Why anybody would want to hurt Eddie beats the hell out of me."

"Sounds like you knew her pretty well."

He hunched his shoulders, then let them drop. "'Bout as much as anybody in here. We all liked her. She was lots of fun, and a great singer."

"Did she ever talk about her husband?"

"Once in awhile," he said, his tone guarded.

"I got the impression myself that they were having some problems."

"Could be. That wasn't none of my business."

"Of course not. I do know the guy was working a lot of overtime."

"Leaving her alone in an empty flat every night," Voyczek remarked. "No wonder she came in here so often. The radio is only so much company."

"Yeah. Empty homes can be damned lonely. I know, I've had that experience. How about you?"

"Mine might as well be empty," he said without feeling, making circles on the bar with a fingertip.

"Sorry to hear that."

Another shrug. "My problem, nobody else's. I'll keep living with it. Have for years."

"As my old Czech grandmother used to say, 'nobody ever promised that life was going to be a stroll in the park with violins playing.'"

That brought the trace of a smile from Voyczek. "And *my* old Czech grandmother, who we lived with for years over on Sacramento when I was growing up, used to get all dramatic and say 'Well, that's it; we're all going to the poor house' whenever the mailman delivered a bill. Yet when she died, we found out she had over thirty grand stashed in about six different accounts in the building and loans along Cermak Road. Nobody in the family ever figured out where she got it all, but nobody in the family objected when they got a piece of it, either."

"Maybe she robbed banks on the side."

"Or building and loans along Cermak Road," he

responded, again with the hint of a grin.

"I've got a question," I said. "Just for the sake of argument, let's assume that my cousin Charlie did not kill his wife. Do you have any idea who might have?"

"Why ask me? She was related to you."

"That's true, at least by marriage, but I really didn't know her very well, not nearly as well as all of you in here. I only saw her a couple of times, when my wife and I had them over for dinner."

He rubbed his chin with a calloused hand. "'Fraid I got no idea. Sounds like you're desperate to find somebody that the law can finger."

"Maybe so," I conceded. "All I know is that Charlie Malek is no killer."

"Seems from what I've read and heard, the cops think he is."

"Yeah, I've talked to a few cops about it myself. I know 'em from my line of work with the insurance companies."

"What do they tell you?"

"That they think maybe they've got their man. But there's a lot of heat on them right now, what with the Degnan murder and all."

He made a face. "They trying to pin that one on your cousin, too?"

"Wouldn't surprise me. Hey, you were probably in here last Wednesday night, the night Edwina was killed. See anything that seemed–I don't know–different? Or anybody who was acting funny?"

Voyczek screwed up his square face in thought. "Wednesday, let's see...Oh yeah, that was the night I had to mend a leak in the water heater in the basement of our six-flat. I'm the only guy in the building that knows how to fix anything. The landlord, he's worthless. Anything tougher than changing light bulbs, and he's out of his depth."

"So you didn't stop by here at all that night?"

"Nope. The damned water heater took me until close to eleven-thirty to fix. By then, I was too damned beat to feel like going any place."

"Can somebody vouch for you all that time?"

"I don't–hey, what the hell is that supposed to mean?" he snapped, lifting off his stool.

"Just a question."

"Well, I don't like the question, Malek. Who do you think you are, accusing me of..." He didn't finish the sentence, but he did keep glowering at me, his fists clenched on the bar.

I held up a palm. "Hey, I didn't accuse you of anything, but you might want to think about whether anybody saw you that night, particularly in the early part of the evening, say around six to seven-thirty or so. The police may very well start rethinking Edwina's murder."

"Damn you! You're willing to do anything to save your pathetic cousin's ass, aren't you? Eddie thought he was..."

"Was what?"

The increasing heat of our dialogue caused heads to turn in our direction. "Everything all right here?" Maury asked.

"Fine, just fine. We're having ourselves a little discussion," I told him.

"Well, we have always prided ourselves on running a peaceful, friendly establishment, *Mister* Malek," the bartender and part owner said pointedly. "And we would all like it to stay that way."

"I couldn't agree more," I responded as the bartender pivoted, answering a bellow for bourbon from the far end of the bar.

"Now, what were you saying about Edwina?" I quietly asked Voyczek.

"Nothin'. Forget it."

"She didn't much like her husband, did she?"

"Look, Malek, I said all that I'm going to say to you."

"No, you haven't. I'm not done yet. I think you were in love with Edwina."

He generated a new glower in my direction. "That's really none of your damn business."

"I suppose not. But finding who killed Edwina–now that I happen to have made my business. And if you were passionate about her, who's to say that passion didn't take a wrong turn last Wednesday night?"

Voyczek scowled. "I don't have to sit here and listen to this crap."

"No, and since you were here first, I'll go and leave you in peace. However, you might keep thinking about what I said. You had better find witnesses who can swear that you were somewhere on Wednesday night other than the apartment of Mr. and Mrs. Charles Malek. Good night."

CHAPTER 15

After the usual spirited chatter in the pressroom to kick off Wednesday morning, I made my way, also as usual, down one flight to the office of Detective Chief Fergus Fahey. "And how are you this fine morning, Mr. Malek?" Elsie Dugo Cascio bubbled as I strode into her minuscule anteroom.

"Just what gives you the right to be so cheerful so early in the day?" I muttered with mock grumpiness.

"Oh dear, did we have ourselves a long night?" she said, putting on her most sympathetic face. "And in answer to your question, I'm always cheerful when I see you. You brighten my little corner of the world just by showing up every day."

"You take all the fun out of being a grouch," I replied, trying without success to stifle a smile.

"That's what I'm here for—to take the grouchiness out of grouches."

"Well, you've got your hands full with the man in there," I said, gesturing to the closed door. "He's a prime candidate for the Grouches' Hall of Fame."

"Speaking of the man in there, he said you were to

just go right in when you got here."

"Without even knocking?"

"Without even knocking."

"I'll be damned. Is the fine old gentleman getting mellow in his twilight years?"

"Don't let him hear the words 'twilight years'," she said. "He's sensitive enough about his age as it is."

"As well he should be. But those words shall not pass my lips again," I told her as I opened the door to Fahey's cluttered office.

"Reporting on time," I told him, dropping into one of his guest chairs.

"Morning, Snap," he said, looking up from an official-looking sheet he was holding. "I've got some good news for you, of a sort."

"What sort?" I asked as we both lit up Luckies from the pack I had tossed onto his blotter. Just then, Elsie entered with a steaming mug of coffee, which she set down on the corner of the desk in front of me. Fahey waited until she left and had closed the door behind her.

"Your cousin has been cleared of the Degnan murder," he said. "It has been substantiated that he was at work during the time when she was abducted."

"Well, I guess that's something," I remarked, "although as far as I'm concerned, the Degnan thing was never in question as far as Charlie was concerned."

"Right now, you ought to be happy with small favors," Fahey observed.

"Maybe. Fergus, as I think I mentioned earlier, I've been visiting that bar in Pilsen, Horvath's by name, where Edwina Malek spent a lot of evenings while her husband was working overtime for the gas company. As I also mentioned to you before, it seems there were a lot of guys there interested in her, and it also seems from what I've been able to ascertain that she didn't exactly discourage them."

"Your point being?"

"My point being that she apparently was something of a tease, and that she may well have been leading one or more of these guys on. One of them might just have gotten the idea that she was easy and tried something at their apartment while Charlie was out earning time-and-a-half. She held this guy off and maybe ran to the kitchen to get a knife. They fought with it and..." I turned a palm up.

Fahey ground out the cigarette in his ashtray. "Ever thought of writing detective fiction, Snap?" he asked. "That is one of the most convoluted, improbable scenarios that I've ever heard. You're really, really reaching now."

"Hey, I don't think that's such a reach."

"And just how do you propose to get one of these lounge lizards to confess?" he snorted.

"I haven't figured that out," I conceded. "Besides, I've only talked to two of the four gents who supposedly had the hots for Edwina."

"Snap, the very fact that the dead woman was apparently a flirt who led guys on actually works against your cousin's case. What better incentive to get violent with a wife than to learn she's cheating on you–or at least acting as if she's cheating? Besides, you know damn well I don't like the idea of your conducting your own investigation."

"Hey, please feel free to send some of your men to Horvath's to start really questioning these guys. I can supply their names. Shit, why don't you send that hotshot dick of yours, Jack Prentiss, over there to hammer away at them? He's tough as nails, right? Maybe he can pry something out of one of them. I know somebody from the department was in there right after the murder, but whoever it was–maybe Prentiss himself–just asked a few questions and left. That's hardly what I'd term a thorough investigation."

"Actually, that was Prentiss," Fahey fired back. "The reason he went in there was because a neighbor suggested it was something of a hangout for the dead woman. He found out from the bartender that she was a regular–and the most popular person in the joint to boot."

"So after this so-called in-depth interview with the barkeep, he left satisfied that Charlie Malek must have been the one to kill this personable, charming woman."

"Ease off, Snap. Hellfire, you've already done your cousin one good turn by hiring the best damn defense lawyer in town for him. Let McCafferty deal with this. That's his business, for God's sake."

"Even with McCafferty in Charlie's corner, it's a crap

shoot, Fergus. It's too chancy."

Fahey leaned back and took a drag on his cigarette. "So, what are you going to do next?"

"I've identified four of the Horvath habitués who were particularly *fond*, shall we say, of Edwina Malek. I've already talked to two of them, and I plan to visit with the other two, one at a time."

"I don't like it."

"As I said, you're welcome to send somebody else over there, even Prentiss again, although I'm going to talk to these others myself anyway."

"Listen, with the murders of the Degnan girl and those two women, my manpower is already stretched so thin that I've got dicks working double shifts."

"So what choice do I have, if I want to get my cousin out of this goddamn mess he's in? Fergus, you really think he's guilty, don't you?"

The grizzled copper fixed his light blue eyes on me.

"Have you ever known me to work against the best interests of the department, or the public?"

"No, I haven't."

"Have you ever known me to bullshit you?"

"No, again."

"Well, I'm not about to start now. To answer your question…yes, from everything I've read in the reports and heard, I believe that your cousin killed his wife. But that's not for me—or you—to decide, as you know very well. That's why we've got courts. Now, I can't stop you from going out and conducting your own rogue investigation, although I strongly advise against it.

"For some strange reason that I've never bothered analyzing, I like you, Snap. I haven't said that to very many other newspapermen over the years—none, that I can recall. But you've grown on me like a barnacle on the hull of a ship. And there's enough trouble in your family now without you going out and mixing it up with a bunch in some second-rate Pilsen saloon. I've seen enough of bar fights to know how tough some of these guys can be—I had to break up a few of those set-tos in my days on the street. I took a few punches, but I gave as good as I got." He leaned back and put his arms behind his head, a signal that he was about to reminisce.

"I remember once, my partner Mulroy and I had to put down a brawl in a gin mill in Englewood, on Halsted a few blocks south of 63rd, it was. I can still remember it like yesterday—place called Herlihy's.

"This miserable excuse for a saloon was always giving the precinct headaches—slugfests two, three nights a week. The lieutenant was fed up to here. Well, this one time, we decided we'd had enough. We walked in there in the middle of a melee and Mulroy, he was a big, burly former wrestler, picked up one of the scrappers over his head and threw him through the air against the back bar.

"At least ten bottles, some of them the best whiskey in the place, ended up broken, as well as the big plate glass mirror behind them. And the guy who got tossed, a mean little bastard, was pretty well cut up and got himself a broken arm out of it. The barkeep went wild, said that we were destroying his establishment."

"Which you were, of course."

Fahey allowed himself a slight smile. "Not really. We dared him to make a stink about it, telling him that if he tried to claim we'd done it, we'd just say that's the way we found the place when we walked in. We knew damn well that the lieutenant would back us all the way. The upshot was that we never had to go back in there to break up another fight. It became a nice, peaceful corner bar after that."

"That must have been way back when, in the dark ages before Prohibition," I said with a grin.

"Okay, so I'm no spring chicken. Yep, that was just before the Volstead Act kicked in, back in '19, but bar life isn't all that different today. There's always somebody in a dive who's spoiling for a fight. We still see it all the time."

"But in all the years I hung out at Kilkenny's up on North Clark, I never once saw so much as a scuffle. Well, except for the time back in '38 when Dizzy Dean bailed me out of a tight spot by bouncing a fastball off the noggins of a couple of hoods. Don't believe I ever told you about that episode."

"No, as a matter of fact you didn't. But you're making my very point for me," Fahey said. "Wherever you go, trouble has a way of following close behind. You could walk into the most peaceful bar in the whole damn state, and before long there'd be a brawl or, at the very least, a shoving match."

"But Fergus, I am the most peace-loving of men," I told him, holding up my hands in innocence.

"Right, and I am just a humble parish priest, ministering to my flock. Snap, far be it from me to suggest you're a troublemaker by nature, but you have to admit that you seem to find ways to get yourself into scrapes."

"All in the line of duty and in the pursuit of the forces of evil," I said in my best radio-announcer voice.

"Or in the pursuit of scoops," the chief remarked dryly.

"Normally, I would agree with you on that point, Fergus, but that's not what's driving me this time around, as I think you know."

"Yeah, blood relations count for a lot, as I'm aware. You just have to be careful that they don't blind you to realities."

"If I didn't think Charlie was clean on this, I wouldn't be making such a big deal out of it, Fergus. You know me well enough to realize that."

"I just don't know what else to tell you," Fahey said, throwing his hands up in a gesture of futility. "You're going to do whatever you want to anyway. All I can say is, for God's sake be careful, will you?"

"Fergus, I promise to proceed with all due caution. I've grown increasingly fond of myself over the years, and I would like to hang around for a few more decades."

"Well, that's more time than I'll be allotted," the chief grumbled, putting his head down and leafing through a stack of reports as the signal that I had been dismissed.

"Wait a minute," I said as I started to get up. "There's something you can do that won't put much of a strain on your overburdened staff."

"Yeah?" He looked at me, dubious.

"I'll give you the names of these four guys from the bar, and you can get somebody in Records to run a check on them. That way, we'll at least know something more about their backgrounds. Might bring some interesting stuff to light."

"Sounds to me like a fishing expedition," Fahey snorted.

"As an old fisherman, you know that you can't catch anything without dropping your line into the water," I replied.

"Okay, Snap, I'll humor you on this one," he said, "but only because we go back a long way."

"That we do," I agreed, writing down the names of the four on a sheet from my notebook. I tore it out and handed it to Fergus.

He took it from me and went back to studying the top report on his stack of paperwork.

I had not been back at my desk in the pressroom for more than five minutes when I got a call from Liam McCafferty.

"Mr. Malek, I believe that I have some felicitous news for you," he said in the melodic brogue that had mesmerized so many juries through the years. "It pleases me to tell you that your cousin is no longer under suspicion regarding the tragic murder of Suzanne Degnan."

"Thanks for the call. In fact, I just heard the same news myself here."

"Ah! You would, of course, given the place where you toil. Well, it was a ridiculous suspicion in the first place. Totally ridiculous, but as we both know, the police are under a great strain over that poor girl's killing. In any event, this is one less particular we need to concern ourselves about at this time."

"Well and good, and I thank you for the call. I'm more interested, however, in your thoughts about the murder that he *is* charged with, counselor."

"As am I, obviously. I have nothing new and, in fact, I was telephoning you to see if you had discovered anything in your own investigations."

"Not really. I have talked to two of the four men who regularly frequent Horvath's and who were known to have had more than a passing interest in the late Mrs. Malek. You'll be interested to learn that neither one has an alibi for the period when she was killed. I still plan on seeing the other two in the next few days, with luck. Have you been to see Charlie again?"

"No. For the moment, I believe I am in possession of

all the information that he is able to supply me. Or, I should say, that he deems able to supply me."

"I want an honest answer: Assuming the case were to be tried today, what do you think Charlie's chances would be?"

A pause followed, then McCafferty cleared his throat. "A great deal would depend upon the composition of the jury," he intoned somberly.

"But you have a great deal of influence on that composition, right, counselor?"

"I do what I can, given my modest talents."

"Well, then let's assume for the sake of discussion that you get precisely the jury you want."

"If that were the case—and it can be a big 'if'—I believe it is fair to say that I would feel considerable confidence about the outcome."

I didn't believe him, of course, dismissing his comment as the perpetual optimism of a defense attorney. I thanked him, however, saying I would let him know about my further investigations, then hung up and mused on the ability of lawyers to spout fine phrases and say almost nothing in the process.

CHAPTER 16

I knew that I was rapidly wearing out my welcome at Horvath's Tap, if I even had one to begin with, but I had resolved to push on and decided to alter the pattern. That is, I would just show up at the saloon tonight and not make any prearrangements with Marge Blazek. I didn't want it to look like she and I were working together. If she happened to be in there, fine, if not, also fine. I'd figure out how to meet Len Rollins and Johnny Sulski all by myself.

At just after seven-thirty, I stepped into the haze and headed across the rarely used dance floor to an empty stool at the left end of the bar. One or two men turned to look in my direction as I walked across the room, and Ben Barnstable once again grinned and gave me a nod before turning back to his drink. Neither Marge nor Karl Voyczek were in attendance.

Maury, who seemed to be the only bartender on the payroll, scowled in my direction, clearly wishing that I'd chosen some other watering hole. "Schlitz on draught, as usual," I said with a grin.

"If I remember from your description the other night,

that's Rollins down at the far end of the bar, right?" I asked when he set the chilled glass of lager on a coaster in front of me.

He scowled some more. "Yeah, that's him with a plaid jacket on," he said in a voice just above a whisper. "Are you plannin' to cause any trouble in here tonight?"

"Me, trouble? Not at all, Maury, and I'm surprised you would ask. I'm the peace-loving type all the way. Buy Mr. Rollins a drink, whatever his pleasure is, and tell him that it's on me. Put it on my tab, of course."

He shrugged and walked down to the far end of the bar. I nursed my Schlitz, waiting. I was half finished with it before Maury came back.

"He says thanks for the drink and wants to know why you bought it for him."

"Fair question. Ask him if he minds coming down here so that we can talk. Then he can find out for himself why I'm so generous."

"I ain't used to being anybody's messenger boy," the barkeep huffed.

"But it's all part of your role as a gracious host, Maury." He grimly stomped off, shaking his head and muttering, presumably to give Rollins my message.

About five minutes later, a short, watery-eyed specimen of about forty-five with Dagwood Bumstead-style black hair and wearing a plaid woolen jacket shuffled over to me, highball in hand.

"You the guy who bought me the drink?" he asked,

his voice slightly slurred.

"I'm the one," I told him. "Pull up a stool and join me."

"I don't know you, do I?" he said, squinting at me as he sat down.

"Nope. I'm fairly new around here. You been a customer of Maury's for a long time?"

He nodded, contemplating what was left of his drink. "Yeah, buncha years now. Nice place, huh?"

"Sure seems to be. Good folks. I imagine that you must know a lot of them after all this time, eh?"

"Oh, yeah, a lot of 'em. Good guys, good guys."

"It's Len, right? I'm Steve."

"Yeah, Len Rollins. Nice to meetcha, Steve." He cast another glance at his disappearing drink.

"Two more down here, Maury," I called out to be heard over the din of conversation and jukebox. "We're getting kind of dry at this end."

I turned to Rollins. "What do you do for a living, Len?"

"I work the day shift on the loading docks south of here, near the canals," he said in a deprecatory tone. "Just a job."

"Honest work," I commented. "There's nothing wrong with that."

"Guess not," he replied as Maury placed fresh drinks in front of us. "Been doin' it for years, ever since I was a kid just outta high school."

"Did you know the woman from in here who got killed?" I asked off-handedly.

"Eddie? Yeah. Sure did." His voice got husky.

"Really sad."

"Husband killed her. Bastard."

"So I've been told. Do they know it was him that did it for sure?"

"Cops think so. They got him in the cooler, so I heard and read in the papers."

"Why would he have done it?"

"Beats the shit outta me. Eddie was a real doll, a honey. We called her Eddie, but her real name was Edwina. She was from England. I loved to hear her talk, and I loved to hear her sing, too. Did she ever have a voice? Knew all kinds of songs."

"Sounds as if you liked her a lot."

Rollins nudged his glass around on the bar with an index finger. "I sure did. She cheered me up, even made me laugh sometimes, and I ain't what you'd exactly call a laugher. She came over here to be with…him, after the war. One of them war brides, you know? God damn, she moves all the way to our good ol' U.S.A. to find a new life and look how she ends up." I thought he was going to start crying.

"Doesn't seem fair."

"Damn right it doesn't."

"Pardon me for repeating my question, but why would her husband want to kill her, do you think?"

He turned in my direction, trying to bring me into focus. "Okay, you want my opinion? I think he was jealous of her, that's what I think."

"Jealous, huh? Why?"

"Because she had all these friends in here. All these people who liked to be around her. She was the best thing that ever happened to this here joint."

"Men? Women? Who were these friends?"

Rollins chewed his lower lip, as if trying to think. I figured I had about ten, maybe fifteen minutes before his brain ceased to function in any logical fashion.

"'Most everybody in the place. They all liked her, all of 'em, all of 'em."

"Anybody special come to mind for you, Len?"

"The big guy for one, he's down that way." He gestured vaguely toward the other end of the bar, where Barnstable had parked himself.

"Who's that?"

"Ben. Big Ben, they call him. The ol' boxer. Good fella, heart o' gold. Great guy. You'd like him. Yeah, really great guy."

"Who else, Len?"

He frowned, working to concentrate. "Ya got ol' Karl, he woulda killed for her, I think. God, he really liked her."

"Would you say that he loved her, Len?"

"Loved her? Geez, I dunno, maybe. Sure."

"And you think he actually would have killed for her?"

"I didn't really mean that," he said, as flustered as someone in his condition could be.

"No, I didn't think you meant it. You were just using an expression. Besides the boxer fellow and this Karl, was there anybody else particularly who was friendly with the lady?"

"Well, yeah, there was Sulski, for sure. He was really interested in her."

"Romantically interested?"

He raised his shoulders and let them drop. "I just know that he liked her a lot. Sulski, he was sort of jealous of anybody else who talked to her. He always tried to sit next to her when she came in. Even reserved a stool for her and wouldn't let anybody else sit on it."

"Did that make the rest of you angry?"

"Aw, I dunno. None of us is really the fightin' type, I guess, not even Big Ben, and hell, that's what he used to do for a living," he said, taking a healthy swig of his drink. "He could prob'ly knock any of us out with one punch, but like he says now, he quit using his fists the very day he left the ring."

I hadn't told Rollins what my relationship to Edwina was and didn't plan to unless he got curious, which seemed unlikely, given his current state. "So Barnstable, Voyczek, and Sulski all were cozy with the lady–or wanted to get cozy with her. Did she have any other friends in here?"

"Well, she was always joking with Maury, of course,

but then we're all pals with him. Good ol' Maury. Best bartender in Chicago. Great guy, great guy. Then there's Marge, she and Eddie used to sit together a lot, talking and laughing."

"Marge?"

"Yeah, she comes in here a lot. Haven't seen her yet tonight, though."

"What's she like?"

"Nice gal, real nice. Lost her husband in the war, in that big D-Day battle it was. Sometimes, she gets real sad, anybody could tell it. Hard to blame her though, huh?"

"Yes, it is hard to blame her. Good looking woman, is she?"

"Yeah, I'll say, a real peach. She's got a great figure, too."

"Then I suppose that some of the guys were pretty sweet on her as well as on Eddie, eh?"

"Well, they woulda been–me, too, I guess–except Marge, she just don't act like she's all that interested in goin' out with guys right now. Still probably in a period of mourning, leastways that's how I see it."

"So it probably didn't bother her that all of you paid so much attention to Eddie, right?"

Rollins waved my question away. "Nah, she wasn't the jealous kind. She wouldn't care even if we'd been drooling all over Eddie. And sometimes it damn near seemed like Sulski was. Drooling, I mean."

He let out a sound somewhere between a snort and a

laugh, then stiffened up, and shook his head. "Sorry. I shouldn't be talking like that about somebody who's dead. That ain't decent."

"That's okay, Len. I know that you meant no disrespect."

"Nah, not for Eddie. I'd never say anything bad about her. She was always real nice to me. God, I'm so sad." He sniffled and dabbed at his eyes with an index finger, turning away from me.

"Well, I know it's got to be a bad time for everybody who knew her. She must have died just about this time a week ago. Were you in here when you found out about it?"

"In here?" He screwed up his face. "No…no I wasn't. That night, I didn't come in here till later. Guy I work with named McMannis bought me a drink and a steak sandwich at a diner over on Loomis near where our loading dock is. He was payin' off a bet we made on the Zale-Hughes fight down Texas way. Mac, he really thought that palooka Hughes would win, but Tony knocked him out in the second round. For me, the bet was like takin' candy from a baby."

"That must be quite a walk back here from Loomis, huh?"

"Not so bad, maybe forty-five minutes or so," he muttered, unaware that he was being cross-examined.

"When I got back here, I sorta wondered why Eddie wasn't around. None of us in here, we didn't find out till the next day what had happened to her." He started to sniffle again.

I tried to think of something solicitous to say, but before anything came out, the door opened and the guys at the bar turned to acknowledge the new arrival. "Hey, there she is," Len Rollins told me. "The one I was talking about. That's Marge."

"Oh, yes, I recognize her from when I was in here before," I told him. "Hi, there," I said, dipping my chin in her direction. "Nice to see you again."

She picked up on my line like a good actress. "Oh, hello, how are you?" she said with just the proper amount of disinterest. She found a spot at the other end of the bar while I turned back to Rollins.

"Well, I'd better be going. I've got a long day tomorrow," I told him as I settled up my tab with Maury, who clearly was happy to see me go.

"Thanks for the drinks. 'Preciate it, fella," Rollins slurred.

"My pleasure," I replied, as happy as I'd ever been to have a good job and a loving wife to go home to.

CHAPTER 17

In the pressroom at Headquarters the next morning, I had barely got settled with a copy of the three-star final and a Lucky when my phone jangled. It was Marge Blazek.

"I was surprised to see you show up last night," she said in a concerned tone. "You never called yesterday to say you were going to be at Horvath's, like you did the other times."

"Sorry about that. I got to feeling bad that you were staying away from your favorite hangout because of me. Thought I'd do things a little differently this time."

"I see that you got to talk to Len. How did that go?"

"Okay, I guess. He sure likes the sauce."

"Yeah, he does hit it pretty hard, all right. You've seen them all now except Johnny."

"Yeah, seems like he must not be coming in all that much. I have yet to see him."

"Oh, he showed up last night all right, 'bout an hour or so after you left. I asked him where he'd been hiding himself, and he said he's been kind of down after...well, you know."

"After Edwina."

"Yeah. Anyway, I told him it was good to have him back. Says he'll be there again tonight."

"I will be too. Please don't stay away on my account. I can always get Maury to finger him for me."

"You know I'll be glad to help any way I can."

"I know that, and I appreciate it. How about describing Sulski to me, in case Maury isn't all that cooperative? He's getting damn tired of me coming in and asking him questions."

"Johnny, he's, well, sorta light-haired, not exactly blond, but close to that. Medium height, I guess; I usually see him sittin' down. And stocky, but not fat. He doesn't talk much, he's maybe even quieter than Rollins. He's got a square face and he doesn't smile hardly at all. Except that Eddie, she could get him to smile, and even laugh, which is more'n I could ever hope to do. I think he sees himself as a tough guy."

"The strong, silent type, huh?"

"Pretty much, yeah. That's a good way to put it."

"Sounds like Edwina was able to break through that pose of his though, huh?"

"Yeah, she did. Hey, sorry, I gotta go now–a customer just walked in the door."

I thanked her and told her I'd be on my own at Horvath's tonight.

The rest of the day dragged as if I were in my dentist's chair getting a root canal. I made my regular visit to

Fergus Fahey's office, where the big news was that Elsie had announced her pregnancy.

"That's just terrific!" I said, giving her a squeeze. "I always knew that you had it in you."

"Now I really have it in me," she shot back, smirking prettily and patting her still-flat stomach.

Fahey was less enthused about her condition when the two of us got settled in his office.

"Best damn secretary a man could want, and now I'm going to lose her," he grumbled after taking a drag on one of the cigarettes I had supplied. "God knows how I'll ever fill those small but very large shoes of hers."

"You'll find a way, Fergus. How long has she been working for you now?"

"Eight, maybe nine years, since she was fresh out of high school. She caught on to things around here right away; I never had to tell her anything twice. Seemed to always anticipate what I need. My wife says Elsie was the third-best thing that ever happened to me—after her and the kids, of course."

"Well, I have to admit she's a gem, all right. But it was only a matter of time before somebody else found that out. I was surprised that somebody hadn't grabbed her sooner."

Fahey leaned back and considered me through narrowed eyes. "I always thought that somebody might've been you."

"Honestly, Fergus, it never crossed my mind," I told

him, taking a sip of Elsie's superb coffee. "It's just that I guess neither one of us ever thought of the other in that way."

"That's where you've got it wrong, Snap. Elsie had it bad for you at one time, really bad...but by God, you never heard that from me, right?"

"Right," I replied, honestly surprised, at least in part because I was more than fifteen years older than the lovely little brunette who was typing in the outer office.

"Well, it's all past history now," he said, blowing a cloud of smoke. "She's happily married, and by all accounts you are as well, I gather."

"Yes, I am. I almost let this one get away a few years ago, but I came to my senses somewhere along the line. Nice when we're given second chances; I'm damn happy for Elsie."

"In truth, I am, too, of course," the old cop said. "She told me that she's planning to come back in a few months, but I don't believe that for a minute. I also don't think she should come back...just call me traditional."

"That's something we agree on, Fergus. But, God, I'm going to miss her coffee."

"She's promised to train her replacement in what I consider the fine art of brewing," he said, "but she'll never be able to train someone to be like her in lots of other ways that nobody could hope to explain."

"Agreed again. In there anything that we need to talk about on my beat?"

"Quiet day so far," he replied. "What about you?"

"Same."

"Still searching for someone to take your cousin's place in that cell at the Bridewell?"

"Yes I am, Fergus. I know you don't much like to hear that, but what else can I do?"

He released a world-weary sigh and shook his head slowly. "Just don't become part of the news yourself, okay?"

"Okay," I said with a grin, getting up and leaving. "See you around."

At the dinner table that evening, I told Catherine I would be making another visit to Horvath's.

"Is this really getting you somewhere, Steve?" she asked as she served me tuna casserole. "From what you've told me so far, I can't see that you've really learned anything."

"Except that none of the three guys I've talked to has an alibi for the time Edwina was killed."

"But what does that prove?"

"That any one of them could have done it."

"I know this is hardly my métier, but it seems to me that you've got to have both evidence and motive for the killing. Where are they?"

"There may never be any hard-and-fast evidence," I conceded. "As to motive, they all supposedly lusted after her to varying degrees. What I'm trying to find out is whether one of these guys, in his lust, tried to force himself on Edwina at her and Charlie's apartment and a scuffle started, with her ending up getting knifed in the chest."

Catherine nodded, lips pursed. "Just where do you stand with that?"

"Nowhere, yet. I've got one more guy to talk to, and he's supposed to be at Horvath's tonight."

"I don't mean to sound like a cross-examining attorney in a courtroom, Steve, but what if you don't get anything out of this last man? Then what?"

"I've got to persuade the cops to grill all four of them until one cracks."

"But you've said that your friend the chief isn't inclined to do that."

"I'll figure out a way to talk him into it, somehow. Along those lines, by the way, I've asked him to see if any of these guys have records."

"And you still remain absolutely convinced that Charlie couldn't have done it?"

"Absolutely, unequivocally."

She lifted her shoulders and let them drop. "I know it's fruitless to try to talk you out of going to that bar tonight. But you've got to promise me that you'll be careful. Things could get out of control."

"I promise. If anything happened to me, that would hardly help Charlie's cause, would it?"

CHAPTER 18

I left for Pilsen early because I wanted to take a detour before hitting Horvath's. I turned down a quiet block of 19th Street and cruised by the building where I was born. I hadn't seen the place in the half-dozen years since my parents had died within a few months of each other, and I was curious as to how it looked.

Everything looked the same—why wouldn't it—except that whoever lived there now had a different lamp in the living room window, an ornate gold thing with an oversized shade that filled the window. I preferred my mother's red-and-blue Tiffany, which my sister Marcia had now. Marcia lived in a bungalow in Downers Grove with her husband, an auto mechanic named Matt, who was a decent sort, if a little on the dull side. They had two kids, Betsy and Matt Jr., both of whom were in high school.

I hadn't seen much of Marcia and her family since the folks died—no particular reason—but since we'd been married, Catherine thought we should get together with them occasionally, like on holidays. So we had begun to, which was all right, I guess.

It was raining when I drew the coupe to the curb on

the side street off of 18th that ran next to Horvath's. The joint was less crowded than I'd seen it before, so there were plenty of open stools.

"How long you gonna keep coming in here?" Maury said in a tired voice after I sat down.

"There you go again, not being as hospitable as you should," I chided. "You are the host in here, the face of this establishment. How in the world do you expect to get new business with that kind of attitude?"

"There's some business I can very nicely do without, thanks."

"Well, I guess I've been told. But I'll pretend I didn't hear that comment and request a Schlitz."

As Maury shuffled off, I looked along the bar, but found no one who looked like Marge's description of Sulski. Karl Voyczek, who sat several seats from me engrossed in reading a copy of the evening tabloid, *The Times*, was the only familiar face present.

I nursed my beer for more than a half hour and contemplated ordering another when the door swung open and a blocky, light-haired specimen in a black coat and a pugnacious expression walked in. This had to be Sulski.

"Hey, Johnny," a guy halfway along the bar called out, "how's it going, big guy?"

Sulski grunted his reply and made for a barstool two removed from me, with no one between us. He dropped onto the seat like he planned to stay awhile.

"Evening," I said, hoisting my glass in his direction. I

received the second grunt he'd uttered since entering.

"Still raining?" I persisted. His third grunt sounded like it could have been a yes.

"Have the usual, Johnny?" Maury said, getting a nod in answer. He put a highball in front of Sulski that looked to be scotch and soda.

I ordered a second beer and turned toward my neighbor. "I'd like to talk to you about Edwina Malek," I told him.

He spun toward me, light blue eyes blazing. "So you're the one, huh? The snoopy type who's been nosing around here lately. I heard about you last night. Just what's your story?"

"Edwina was married to my cousin," I told him, "and I know he couldn't–"

"Yeah, yeah, I heard that part, too, from Maury. Well, goddammit, I hope your miserable cousin fries."

I glared back at him. "Even if he didn't kill her?"

"Oh, don't give us that horseshit in here, Mac. Who the hell else would have done it?"

"Maybe somebody who knew her and, shall we say, got his advances rebuffed."

"What's that supposed to mean?" Sulski snarled, flexing his fists.

"Just what I said, *Mac*. Story is there are a lot of joes who hang out in here that were plenty interested in Edwina. Guys who get interested in women sometimes do strange and violent things. "

"I ought to knock you right through the door and into the middle of next week!"

"Strikes me, Mr. Sulski, that you're reacting strangely for a man who claims that somebody else killed Edwina. Like maybe you're using your anger as a sort of cover for...well, for a guilty conscience."

"Shit, that does it!" he raged, getting up and kicking over the stool that was between us. "I'm going to–"

"Take it easy, Johnny," the bartender urged, leaning across the bar and placing a hand on his bicep. "We haven't ever had any fighting in here as long as I've run the place, and we're not going to start now."

"Well, get him the hell out of here, Maury," Sulski yelled, "or honest to God, I'll kill him! I will–I'll kill him!"

"Interesting word coming from you, kill," I said. Sulski was now being held back by two other men who had jumped off their stools.

"It's really time for you to leave," Maury said, his voice quavering. "Please take your business elsewhere. And there's no charge for your beers."

"No, I insist," I retorted, pulling out my wallet and placing two dollars on the bar–more than I owed. "And, Mr. Sulski, a word of advice: Be careful how you throw around that word 'kill.' Good night." I left with all the dignity that I could muster. I felt that every eye in the place was on me as I pushed the door open and walked out.

But I didn't get far. I was halfway across the side

street toward my car when Sulski came barreling after me like a runaway locomotive.

"You son-of-a-bitch," he yelled, throwing a roundhouse right that glanced off my cheek as I ducked. His second punch caught me in the gut and doubled me over against the side of the coupe.

I could feel the nausea rising within me, but I stifled it and caught him with a left to his Adam's apple. He started to gag and I hit him with a right, this time to his own gut, but he took that punch better than I had, making a puffing sound and counterpunching to my face, once, twice.

I wasn't much of a fighter. What little I had learned about defending myself early on came in this very neighborhood. A chunky Polish kid who I only ever knew as 'Stosh' had tried to keep me from walking down a block of 19th Place, claiming it was 'his street.'

Stosh had pushed me in the chest and I'd shoved him back. Pretty soon we were swinging at each other, with maybe half the punches connecting. I lost the fight that day and ended up with a bloody nose, but I came back a week later and knocked him down about three times after I figured out that he couldn't block rights to his stomach.

I realized that Sulski reminded me of Stosh as I gave him a couple of jabs in the side, one of which spun him around. Before he could react, I got him again with an uppercut to the solar plexus that caused him to retch and double over with a groan.

At this point, I was bleeding over one eye and felt

dizzy. I leaned against the coupe, watching him hold his belly and trying to figure out whether I had the strength–or the inclination–to hit him again.

By this time, half a dozen of the Horvath stalwarts had tumbled out onto the street and were trying to wedge their way between us. "That's enough, fellas," Big Ben Barnstable drawled as he pushed his way in and put a large, vise-like hand on each of our shoulders.

"Good thing I came out jest now, in time to stop this here bout, boys. Now I can't say much good about your form, either one of you," he said good-naturedly, "but if you'd like to take lessons, we've got us this fine gym not too far away where I earn my keep. We've also got us a real good instructor, a former middleweight named Haas. He can work with you, make you look like you know what you're doing with your fists."

That brought a laugh, albeit a nervous one, from the onlookers and effectively sucked the tension out of the moment. Sulski and I glared at each other, but it was clear that glaring was all we were going to do now, especially with the big former boxer standing between us like a brick wall.

The crowd, if you could term it that, all turned and headed back into the bar, including Sulski. I obviously was the odd man out, so I climbed into the Ford, mopped the blood off my eyebrow with a handkerchief, and drove home, frustrated and just plain mad.

CHAPTER 19

First, of course, I had to face the proverbial music at home. One of the many endearing things about Catherine, though, was that "I told you so" does not occupy a pigeonhole in her roll-top desk of phrases.

She was up in the bedroom reading Hershey's "A Bell for Adano" when I got home. "Oh, Steve!" she said, jerking upright in bed as I walked in. "Lord, are you all right?"

"Just a scuffle," I answered. "But you shoulda seen the other bum."

Rather than asking for details, she hustled me into the bathroom and began ministering to the cut over my eye. "Fortunately, it's not big enough to need stitches," she said, "but still, we're going to have to sterilize it. I'm afraid this is going to hurt just a little."

I let out an "ouch" or two as she worked, cleaning off the dried blood, dabbing iodine on the wound, and finally finishing up with a small bandage from the first-aid box she kept in the medicine cabinet.

"Do I really need that thing?" I asked, gingerly running a finger over the bandage.

"Absolutely. We've got to keep the wound clean, and it very definitely is a wound. Do you want to go over what happened?"

So we talked, or rather I did. I gave her the literal blow-by-blow, not leaving anything out. Since she'd already seen the damage, why bother holding back?

"So now what?" she asked with a frown after I finished my narrative.

"I'm giving a lot of thought to Sulski right now," I said. "A guy doesn't act that way unless he's got something to hide–something big."

"But you didn't exactly handle the situation tactfully," she pointed out with irrefutable logic. "You just bore in on him like a bulldozer, which is hardly a way to get information. Based on what you've told me, I'm not surprised that he reacted the way he did."

"It pains me to say it, my darling, but you are absolutely right. I was trying too hard, and I shot off my mouth. This business is getting to me."

"With reason," she conceded, smoothing the bandage gently with a hand. "You've been under a lot of pressure over this horrible business with Charlie."

"Yeah, I guess. Dammit, I just know it has to be one of those four guys. And thanks to my bull-in-a-china-shop approach tonight, I never did find out whether Sulski has an alibi for the night Edwina was killed. Not that he would have told me anyway."

"My advice, oh noble Lancelot, is to get a good

night's sleep," Catherine said, continuing to stroke my brow with a pleasantly cool hand. "Then you can, as Oliver Goldsmith wrote, 'live to fight another day'."

"Oliver Goldsmith? Where do you find all this stuff?"

"Comes from working in a library for years and years," she answered, wrinkling her brow. "You pick up all sorts of things."

"I will have to take your word for it," I said, yawning. "That 'another day' your friend Goldsmith wrote about will come plenty soon enough for me."

The next morning, I had to endure the jibes of my colleagues in the pressroom when they saw my bandage and the eggplant-colored bruise that had developed above my eye.

"All right, Snap. Out with it," Packy Farmer demanded. "Just what happened last night? I thought when you chose to tie the knot again, your carousing, brawling days were well behind you. Seems that I was mistaken."

"Yeah, let's hear it, Malek," Eddie Metz said. "A bar fight? An angry husband? An angry wife—yours, maybe?"

I held up a hand. "I could regale you chaps with any number of exciting tales as to how I came to sport this wound. I will merely tell you that some things defy explanation and this, dear friends and colleagues, is one of them."

"A pretty speech indeed," Dirk O'Farrell snorted. "Is

that the same oration you delivered to your wife last night?"

"Ah, Dirk, I am happy to report that said wife, wonderful helpmeet that she is, not only knows the full story of my battle scars, she also dressed my wounds in a manner worthy of the late, great Florence Nightingale."

"We're happy that you have pulled through," Anson Masters rumbled, "and that you are still able to fulfill your duties here. Speaking of which, it is time for you, sir, indeed for all of us, to make our appointed rounds in search of news to feed the voracious appetites of our hundreds of thousands of readers."

"Hey, Antsy, that's your best bit of morning cheerleading yet," Farmer said. "Almost wants to make a fellow go to work, but not quite."

However, we all did disperse to our respective beats.

"Good morning, mother-in-waiting," I told the comely Elsie as I entered her two-by-four office. "Is the lord of the manor present this fine morning?"

"Before I inquire about your face, I'll remind you that today is Good Friday," she said sweetly. "You will recall that the chief always takes this day off to spend with his family, and to attend mass."

"Right—I should have remembered, especially since my son is coming home from college today for the Easter weekend."

"But do not think that because Mr. F.S. Fahey is away from his office today, he's not working," Elsie cautioned.

Robert Goldsborough

"He has already phoned and dictated three letters to me in the last hour, and I expect several more calls from him. Now, what's the story with your face?"

"'Tis indeed a sad tale and one that I'll not burden you with, save to say that it has nothing whatever to do with domestic strife. In fact, it was my good wife who bandaged me up."

"The warrior home from the battle, licking his wounds, eh? That Catherine of yours sure has to put up with a lot."

"She bears it well. Next time the old gentleman calls in, say that I asked after him and wished him a Happy Easter. And the same to you, young damsel," I said, turning to leave.

"Not so fast, hotshot reporter. Not only is my boss firing off dictation to me from home, he also wants to talk to you."

"This very day? This holy day?"

"Yes, today. In fact, I was about to phone you in the pressroom when you came down to grace me with your presence. The Chief's orders were that you could go into his office and call him at home. Highly irregular, I must say."

"Irregular indeed," I replied, taking the sheet from her on which she had written his home phone number. Sitting at one of the guest chairs in his office, I lit up a Lucky–force of habit in that environment–and dialed. Fahey answered on the second ring.

"Elsie said it was okay to get you on the line," I said by way of apology.

"Yeah, yeah. My wife always wants me home on Good Friday, but somehow my work doesn't also take the day off."

"There are those who might say that you just miss being here where the action is, Fergus."

He grunted. "Interesting crowd you're hanging out with in that Pilsen saloon, Snap. Or at least a couple of them are."

"How so?"

"You asked me to have Records run a check on these guys, as you may recall."

"I thought maybe you'd forgotten, or else just ignored me like you sometimes do."

"Well, I wasn't keen on the idea, I'll say that. But the boys upstairs came up with stuff. You interested in what they got, or are you just on the line to make smart-assed cracks?"

"Fergus, I'm interested, very interested, and I promise, no more cracks."

He cleared his throat. "That'll be the day. First, Len Rollins."

"Yeah, the drunk," I said.

"His imbibing habits aren't mentioned in what I've got," Fahey said testily. "On October 7, 1939, he was involved in a fight during a craps game in a warehouse along the Stetson Canal at 23rd and Loomis. He and one

Jock 'Squirrel' Lenzi got into it during the game, and he stuck Lenzi."

"With a knife?"

"That's usually what you stick someone with," Fahey commented. "Rollins got six months at Stateville for assault with a deadly weapon. It probably would have been longer, but witnesses said that Lenzi actually was the one who started the fight. By the way, once they patched the Squirrel up–the wound was minor–Lenzi got three months himself, for assault."

"Interesting indeed. Anything else worth noting in the report?"

"No, it was just another gambling brawl. We've been getting several of them every weekend for years."

"Any other arrests for our boy Rollins?"

"Nope, that's it. Then there's this Voyczek character."

"Karl the sullen?"

"I'll have to take your word for that. In March 1941, your Mr. Voyczek is supposed to have attacked a 22-year-old legal secretary as she was walking to her home one evening after getting off a streetcar near 16th and Kedvale. He allegedly pushed her into an alley, knocked her down, and tore off most of her clothes. She started screaming, which was heard by some neighbors, and Voyczek ran away before a police cruiser got to the scene."

"Fine, upstanding citizen. And they caught him?"

"In a manner of speaking," Fahey growled. "A

passerby had seen him running a block or two from the scene, and the young woman who was attacked later identified him in a lineup, then changed her mind, saying that she couldn't really be sure it was him."

"Sounds fishy."

"Of course it does! Our men surmised that she had been threatened by Voyczek or one of his brothers–he's got three, and they're a mean bunch. Karl himself is the only one without a record, unless you count this travesty. In fact, one of the Voyczek brothers is in Joliet right now for armed robbery. Knocked over a bank in Berwyn in '42."

"Anything turn up on either Barnstable or Sulski?"

"No, not a thing. And, Snap, the fact that these other two guys are more than just a little shady does nothing to change your cousin's situation, as I'm sure you know."

"Is that so? Let's see, on the one hand we have ourselves a case where a woman was stabbed to death, very possibly by someone with the intent of assaulting her. And on the other hand, we have one man who went to jail for stabbing someone and another man who, by all accounts, assaulted a woman, never mind that he was never brought to trial. One of those might have been a coincidence, but both, Fergus? Aren't you just a wee bit suspicious?"

He grumbled something unintelligible and wished me a Happy Easter.

* * *

After my phone conversation with Fahey, I thought about calling Liam McCafferty to fill him in, but put it off for the time being. I then took advantage of Fahey's absence from his office and the overall lack of newsworthy material from other departments in the building to go out to the Bridewell and see Cousin Charlie.

"How are you bearing up today?" I asked when we were seated on either side of the screen in the drab visitors' room.

He bit his lip. "'Bout the same as before. That lawyer came to see me again, said he's working on my case and that you are, too. Hey, what happened to your face, Stevie?"

"I ran into a guy who didn't like some things I said to him. Actually, he's someone who knew Edwina from that bar, Horvath's."

"Stevie, I don't want you getting into trouble on my account," he said with a frown.

"Well, if I don't poke my nose into this business, who's going to, Charlie? Obviously not the police. This is all part of what McCafferty meant, that I'm working on your case every bit as much as he is, in my own way."

"I just don't want you getting hurt, Stevie," he whined.

"I'll worry about myself. Did Edwina ever talk about the people she met in Horvath's?"

"Not hardly at all, probably because she knew I didn't

like her spending so much time in there."

"Can you remember any names?"

He furrowed his brow. "Let's see...there was a guy named Ben, I think. She mentioned him a couple of times. Called him 'Big Ben,' like that famous old clock in London, you know? I think she said he'd been a professional boxer at one time some years back."

"Anybody else?"

"No. She mainly talked about how friendly everybody in the place was. Told me that going there kept her from being lonesome in the evenings."

"Uh-huh. Anything else you remember about Horvath's, anything at all?"

"That's about it, Stevie. Sorry."

"How're you passing the time in here?"

"It's pretty boring. They do bring us the papers to read, and there are a few magazines."

"Any of the other prisoners bothering you?"

"No, everybody pretty much stays to themselves, except at meals. We do a little talking to each other then, but not too much. And as I told you before, I'm in a cell by myself."

"How about visitors? You had anybody, other than McCafferty, of course?"

Charlie paused a beat before answering. "No, nobody."

"Catherine said to tell you that she's thinking about you and praying about you every day—that is, if you'll accept a prayer from a Universalist."

He made a feeble attempt at a smile. "Oh, that's really nice to hear. Please tell her hi, and that I appreciate it."

"Anything I can bring you next time I come?"

"I can't think of a thing, Stevie. Thanks for asking."

I left him and walked out of the great, gray building, glad to be outside, even though the skies also were gray. As I tried to flag a cab back to Headquarters, I figured that if I ever had to spend time inside those walls, I'd be depressed too. But it seemed to me that Charlie Malek was beyond depressed; he continued to behave like a man who simply did not care what happened to him.

CHAPTER 20

Peter got in from Champaign on the Illinois Central train Friday afternoon. He took the Lake Street El straight to our house, where he would spend the Easter weekend. On most holidays, he alternated his time between Oak Park and the big co-op apartment along North Lake Shore Drive where my ex-wife, Norma, lived with her husband, Martin Baer.

But this particular week, the Baers were vacationing in Biloxi, Miss., which gave me more time with my son. This was just fine as far as Catherine was concerned. She and Peter got along wonderfully, which didn't surprise me, but it did please me. I knew of several divorces where offspring did not take to the second spouses of their parents.

Peter, however, liked both Catherine and Baer. He and Catherine liked to talk about the arts, particularly painting, which generally meant that I was left out of the conversation, having nothing of substance to add. Catherine also was interested in architecture, and the two of them had some spirited discussions about the International School of Design represented by Mies van der Rohe, among others. She was a fan of his work; Peter was not. For the record, I had no opinion.

At Peter's request, I had gotten tickets through our sports department to Saturday afternoon's Cubs-Cardinals game at Wrigley Field, which turned out to be a sellout–40,000 in the stands. As defending National League champs, our Cubs were off to a fast start in the brand new season, sweeping their first three games down in Cincinnati. This was the home opener for the pennant winners, and we had box seats about ten rows behind the Cubs dugout.

Both teams lined up along the foul lines before the game for the opening ceremonies at home plate, which were aired over the public-address system.

"On behalf of the National League, I present to you your championship pennant," League president Ford Frick said to the Cubs manager, Charlie Grimm, handing him the banner at home plate. "I'm supposed to be neutral, so I'm not suggesting that I hope you win it again," Frick said. "But the next time, whoever wins, I hope to present a World Series flag along with it."

"I hope you're here at home plate next year," Grimm said, accepting the flag. A small tractor used by the grounds crew then took the pennant out to the right-field foul pole, where it was hoisted to the top as a band played "God Bless America" and we all sang along.

"This is a piece of history," I told Peter. "Remember it–you may not see anything like it again for awhile."

Unfortunately, when the game started the local boys didn't look like they were the defending champs. They ran into the left-handed St. Louis pitcher Harry "the Cat" Brecheen, who shut them out, 2–0. As the season was to unfold, there was no shame in this…Brecheen went on to win 15 games as the Cardinals won both the National League pennant and the World Series. They defeated the Boston Red Sox and Ted Williams in seven games, with Brecheen tying a World Series record by winning three of the Cardinals' four games.

In spite of the result of our game, both Peter and I had a good time at the ballpark. In what had become a father-son tradition, we had gone to at least one game at Wrigley Field every year since 1938, the year we saw Dizzy Dean pitch against the Yankees in the World Series.

"Well, we didn't win today, Dad, but it was fun just the same," Peter said as we left the ballpark and moved with the crowd toward the Elevated station on Addison Street. "That guy Brecheen looks really tough. Think the Cubs have a chance to take the pennant again this year?"

"I wouldn't hold out a lot of hope. It seems to me that St. Louis and Brooklyn both have better lineups, particularly the Cardinals with Musial, Slaughter, and Moore, along with that good pitching staff of theirs. I hope you don't think I'm disloyal, but I picked our boys to finish only third in the office pool. Where money is concerned—even small amounts—I play with my head and not my heart."

Peter laughed and talked about how, down at the University of Illinois, there were at least as many Cardinal fans as Cubs fans. "These guys from places like Springfield seem to all root for the Cards. Wouldn't you think that they'd be loyal to their home state?"

"Maybe, but Springfield's quite a bit closer to St. Louis than it is to Chicago," I pointed out.

Peter allowed as to how this was true, but it still bothered him. "I'll bet you won't find any Cub fans at the University of Missouri," he countered, and I agreed. We spent the rest of the two El rides back to Oak Park discussing the loyalties of baseball fans around the country.

The three of us had Easter dinner in the dining room of the big stucco house on Scoville Avenue–ham, of course, sliced thin the way I like it. I filled Peter in on my conversation with Frank Lloyd Wright about the possibility of a summer internship for him at Taliesin.

"What's he like, Dad? The profs don't much like him down at school."

"Catherine, give Peter your impression of the great man, and then I'll wade in with my thoughts."

"Well, he certainly doesn't lack in self confidence," she said with a laugh. "He strides around with that cape, hat, and cane like he owns the world. To hear him talk, you'd think he practically invented architecture. And Peter, based on reading about him and hearing him speak that one time, I have to wonder just how difficult he would be to work with. That's something you probably should be thinking about." She turned to me with a "you're next" expression.

"I pretty much agree with that assessment. I'm not qualified to judge his architectural ability; I'll leave that to you and your professors and others who know something about design, although I do like the houses he's built all around this town and I enjoy being in the Unity Temple, even if I don't always understand the church's services as well as I should.

"Regarding his personality…as Catherine says, he seems incredibly opinionated, in particular when it comes to other well-known architects, none of whom he thinks is worth much. Get him going on guys like Mies van der Rohe and this Saarinen fellow, and he's off to the races with his snide comments. He's got one damn big ego, that's for sure. I don't know what he's like to work for, but I, too, can only imagine that he'd be difficult. What do you think of his work?"

Peter finished a slice of lemon pie and wiped his mouth with a napkin. "I like it more than a lot of my profs do, and I also like the fact that he tries to make his buildings blend in with their settings. Maybe that's what he means by 'organic architecture,' which is a favorite term of his. As far as egos, one of my profs claims they all have big ones. 'Show me an architect without an ego, and I'll show you an architect who doesn't have any confidence in his work,' the prof says."

"Do you still think you'd like to work for Wright, even if only for the summer?" I asked.

"Absolutely. What a terrific experience that would be!"

"Given the man's irascibility, the idea of just a summer makes sense," Catherine put in. "That way, you've only made a short-term commitment. You may end up hating the guy."

"I may," Peter said. "But I'm willing to give it a shot. Nothing ventured..."

"Well, if his word is worth anything, I think we may be able to pull it off," I said. "I've talked to Kennedy, the *Trib's* Sunday Editor, and he likes the idea of my doing a long piece on the great man, who, you won't be surprised to learn, is very much the publicity hound."

"Now tell us something that we don't know," Catherine shot back.

"Just so you are aware, Peter," I cautioned, "he seems to have a fairly low opinion of university architectural schools in general."

"Yeah, I've heard that. It may be because he had a bad experience early on as a student up at the U. of Wisconsin, or so I've heard."

"Well, as long as you know what you're getting yourself into."

"Do you mind having to write an article about him?" he asked me.

"No, not at all, son. I think it would be great fun, and

I'll be getting some extra money for doing it as well. He may not like everything I write–in fact, he almost surely won't–but that's okay. And I'm positive I can get some great quotes from others about him."

"Sure, all you've got to do is call some of my profs," Peter chuckled. "On second thought, maybe you'd better not. That could queer the deal for sure."

"Don't worry," I said, "I'll try not to jeopardize your chances to work for a living legend."

"Yeah, a living legend especially in his own mind," Peter said, and we all broke into laughter.

"How's work going?" Peter asked me, changing the subject. "And what's happening with Cousin Charlie? I've been meaning to ask about him ever since I got home."

"Since I wrote you about Edwina's murder, not much has occurred," I answered. "He's still in jail, of course, although I've hired a top defense lawyer for him, name of Liam McCafferty."

"Not much has happened, you say?" Catherine interjected, raising an eyebrow. "I think you ought to tell Peter just what you've been up to these last days."

"Yeah, Dad, fill me in."

"Well, I've been looking into the case a little bit here and there."

Catherine couldn't contain herself. "Peter, 'looking into the case a little bit' is your father's way of saying that he's been playing detective again. You know how he gets. And you must have noticed the bruise over his eye, which you were too polite to ask about." I sent her a glare, but she just shrugged and gave me an unapologetic smile.

Peter set his jaw. "Uh-huh, I did wonder about that bruise. Okay, Dad, come on, out with it."

I was stuck, so I unloaded the whole shebang right there at the dining room table amid the debris of a great Easter feast. I put it all in, from my doubts about Charlie's guilt to my multiple visits to Horvath's and my set-to with Sulski out in the street. I discussed Marge Blazek, Maury the bartender, and the four guys who all seemed to have carried a torch for Edwina. I didn't leave out anything that I thought was pertinent.

And when Peter asked how Charlie had felt about the state of his marriage, I answered as honestly as I could: "I think Charlie knew intellectually that it was over between him and Edwina, but emotionally he just wasn't able to let go of it."

"Well, in the last few minutes I've learned more about this situation than in all our conversations before," Catherine said, pretending to pout. "Peter, you need to come and stay with us more often so that I can find out what's really going on with this guy." She gestured toward me dismissively with her thumb.

"You could've gotten really hurt in that fight," Peter said, his expression somber.

"I know what you're going to say next," I put in with a rueful grin. "That I'm no kid anymore, right?"

He laughed. "You know I would never say such a

thing. Back to the murder...it sounds like you've got several good suspects. The guy who attacked that secretary, for sure, and the one who got into that knife fight. And what about the character–what was his name, Sulski–you butted heads with? Seems like the only one of the four who doesn't sound suspicious is that ex-boxer, Barnstable."

"How about the woman, Marge?" Catherine put in.

"What about her?" I answered.

"What's to say she didn't do it?"

I looked at her and shook my head. "But why? What possible motive could she have?"

"Perhaps she was in love with one of those four guys–Barnstable, if I were to guess–and she figured that if she got rid of her competition in the form of Edwina, maybe he would start paying more attention to her."

"Seems awfully far-fetched," Peter volunteered, "to think that one woman would kill another woman over a man that she had met in some tavern."

"You stole my line, almost verbatim!" I said to my son. "I can't imagine Marge Blazek feeling so strongly about any one of those four that she'd be driven to stick a knife into Edwina."

"Ah, leave it to you males to underestimate the passions of a woman in love," Catherine said with mock solemnity. "Although on reflection, I'm forced to admit that my suggestion is something of a stretch, alright."

She turned toward me. "Based on what you've said

about those four men and their personalities–and their escapades–I would nominate Voyczak as the likely candidate."

"Nah," Peter said, brushing that choice away with a hand. "I'd say it's the one Dad got into the scrape with, Sulski. Sounds like he's got a hair-trigger temper, and that's the kind of person who would end up doing something like what happened to Charlie's wife."

"But wouldn't somebody like that be more likely to kill her with his hands, not with a knife?" I said, playing the devil's advocate.

"True," Catherine said, "but as you mentioned to me the other night, you theorized that whichever of them did the killing might have tried to sexually assault Edwina in her apartment, upon which she ran to the kitchen for a knife to protect herself, and–"

"And there was a struggle, right?" Peter interrupted. "Sure, that's it. They wrestled for the knife, and in the turmoil, she got stabbed. That makes complete sense to me."

"Glad to hear it," I said. "Now to figure out just who did the attacking and the stabbing, and find a way to prove it."

We all looked at one another as though we had question marks over our heads.

CHAPTER 21

On Monday morning, just as I got to the Headquarters pressroom a few minutes before nine, my phone began ringing. "All right, all right, give a guy a chance to at least sit down, will ya?" I yapped at the nagging machine.

The voice on the other end belonged to Elsie Dugo Cascio. "Good morning, sir," she said in an uncharacteristically formal tone. "The chief would like to see you as soon as possible, preferably right now. I've been calling your number every five minutes for the last half hour."

"Hmm. Any idea what he wants?"

"No, he did not choose to share that information with me, but he seemed extremely anxious to see you."

"I am on my way," I told her, trying to dope out what Fahey wanted so early in the workday. It was usually me who was anxious to see him. My first thought was that it had to do with my set-to with Johnny Sulski outside of Horvath's last week. But no laws had been broken, unless someone termed our fight a public disturbance. No cops had been called, at least as far as I was aware.

Maybe it was the bartender, Maury, complaining that

I had threatened him with city inspectors if he didn't cooperate with me. No, that was not likely, either. Maury would hardly have risked even raising the subject, lest it would really bring some inspectors down upon him.

I walked into Elsie's anteroom. "Reporting as requested," I said, saluting smartly and clicking my heels together.

"Go right on in," she replied. "A cup of Nurse Cascio's black nectar soon will follow."

I stepped into the office and Fahey looked up, wearing as grim an expression as I'd ever seen on his big, square, ruddy mug.

"Sit down, Snap," he said gruffly. "Say, what happened to your face?"

"It's a long story, and it can probably wait until you tell me why I'm in here so early in the day."

He nodded and glanced at the sheets he held in his hand. "I've got a story for you and your so-called competitors upstairs. None of this has been released yet. I've been waiting for you."

"Appreciate it. I'm all ears."

"Last night, or rather very early this morning, a few minutes past one o'clock, an individual jumped in front of a Santa Fe Railway freight train near the intersection of Loomis Avenue and 21st Street in Pilsen in an apparent suicide. Are you getting all this?"

I nodded, taking it down in my notebook.

"Good. The dead woman was identified later by a

cousin as Marjorie Blazek Wilson, a war widow." Fahey gave her address in Pilsen.

"Jesus Christ!"

"The dead woman left a note," he continued, "in which she confessed to the murder of another woman, Mrs. Edwina Moreland Malek. In the detailed note, which was found in her purse alongside the railway tracks, she wrote that she had stabbed Mrs. Malek when the two of them argued over a man that they both knew. The handwriting in the note was verified to be Mrs. Wilson's, about two hours ago, by her cousin, Mrs. Gladys Jahns of Lyons, who was the one identifying the body. The details about the killing in the note could only have been known by the murderer."

He looked up at me over his reading glasses. "That's the gist of it."

"How was the cousin…able to identify her?"

"The train didn't actually run over her, as is so often the case. It threw her off to one side," Fahey said, consulting his notes. "According to the medical report, she was barely scarred, other than a large bruise on her head. Apparently the train struck a glancing blow and it was a concussion that killed her. She probably died instantly. Blessedly, she may not have felt much."

"No question that it was suicide?"

"None whatever as far as we are concerned," the chief said. "The locomotive engineer said that she was standing alongside the tracks and at the last moment jumped toward the train. If that isn't enough, you can read the note, which I have here."

I reached for the note, but Fahey pulled it back. "I can't let you take it away–it's evidence, of course, pending an investigation. However, you can read it and copy anything down you want to. But as you'll see, it's quite long. You may not want to…use everything in it."

He carefully set three sheets of light blue, feminine notepaper on the blotter in front of me, as Elsie brought in a cup of coffee, placing it near my right arm.

"The handwriting. It's so neat," I said numbly.

The cop nodded as he lit a cigarette. "That struck me, too. Amazing, isn't it? Here she was, in the last hours of her life, maybe even down to the last minutes, very calmly setting all this out in a hand that surely would have made her old grade school penmanship teacher proud. And filling both sides of all three sheets, almost like an autobiography."

I began reading, and scribbling notes. The longer I read, the colder I became. Marge's tone was very dispassionate, as though she were writing about someone else.

I never thought I'd see a letter that began "To whom it may concern," but there it was, even with the date neatly written in the upper right-hand corner.

I guess I always knew somehow that life would end up badly for me, the missive began. *I don't mean to sound sorry for myself, but from way back, it seems like my plans didn't ever turn out the way I hoped. What I'm saying, what I'm trying to say, should not be taken as any kind of insult to my husband, Dave, who died on that D-Day that was so good for the United States, and so terrible for me.*

Dave knew that he wasn't my first choice, but he was wonderful to me anyway. Very generous. He had wanted for us to have a family–three kids he said, didn't care if they were boys or girls–and a house with a bedroom for each one of them in some nice neighborhood in the suburbs with trees and a yard, and close to a park. He had a town all picked out–Brookfield–and a nice neighborhood not far from the zoo. We even went there once, and he showed me the street he liked and the kind of house he thought would be perfect for us. It was two stories, white, with shutters on the windows and big trees in the front yard.

But that went wrong, like everything else has for me, which I know means I must deserve all that has happened in my life. After Dave was killed, I thought maybe I could go back and change things that occurred before, kind of start over. But...

I continued reading and taking notes as Fergus shuffled through his ever-present paperwork, looking down and saying nothing. Whenever he stopped the shuffling, the only sound in his office was the ticking of the wall clock, and the occasional rattling of an El train as it passed by outside his grimy window.

Marge was far from literary in her style, but her

phrases were poignant: "life at a dead-end," "an aching soul," "the final lie."

I kept reading, and kept being drawn deeper into Marge Blazek's private hell, a hell that ended up taking her own life as well as that of her supposed friend, Edwina Malek. "Part of me really, truly, liked Eddie," Marge wrote in the note, "but another part of me could barely stand the sight of her."

I wrote down everything in the note, word for word, then pushed Margie's handwritten sheets across the desk to Fergus. "I've got everything," I told him.

"Everything?"

"As you said, it's very long. Probably too long to use it all, huh?"

"Far too long to use it all. By the way, this completely clears your cousin, of course. He'll probably get the word at the Bridewell this morning. Great news for him, huh?"

"Yeah. Great news for him."

I took my notes and went back up to the pressroom, where the morning bull session was still in full swing. "I've got some information that I think you'll all be interested in," I told the assemblage. "A woman has confessed to the murder of Edwina Malek, in a suicide note."

"Wow! That's terrific for your cousin. Congratulations!" Packy Farmer boomed, with the others joining in. After that, everybody began talking at once, but I silenced them by slapping a palm down hard on my desk. "Here's the police report and the meat of the suicide note. I'll be happy to read it to you."

They liked that idea–the less work for them, the better, in the fine tradition of Chicago police reporting. Then each of them could fashion his own story. I read the police report and those portions of the suicide note that I chose to select, and they all took notes, with both Farmer and Metz asking me several times, "Slow down, Snap, slow down. For Pete's sake, slow down...we're not goddamn stenographers!"

The process took me about twenty-five minutes, with several interruptions and requests that I repeat some detail or other, and then everybody was on the phone, dictating to their respective city desks.

Because of the timing, the three afternoon papers were out first with the story, and because of the suicide angle, it got bigger play than Edwina's murder had. Both the *Times* and the *Herald American* used it as their banner headline, while the *Daily News*, always more conservative in its coverage of crime news, played the story under a two-column headline on Page 5. The *Trib* and the *Sun* didn't hit the streets with the news until the next morning, in each case running it at the bottom of the front page.

Here, for the record, is what I wrote for the *Trib*:
LOVE TRIANGLE ENDS IN MURDER, SUICIDE
A 26-year-old woman threw herself in front of a
Santa Fe freight train on the Southwest side early
Monday morning, and her suicide note divulged

that she had murdered a friend because of their mutual affection for a man whose identity remains unknown and may never come to light. The dead woman, Margery Blazek Wilson of the Pilsen neighborhood, revealed in a suicide note found near her body that she had fatally stabbed Edwina Moreland Malek, 24, in Mrs. Malek's Pilsen apartment a week ago Wednesday, after they had quarreled. The suicide note made no mention of what specifically had spurred the quarrel.

Mrs. Malek's husband, Charles, a war veteran who had been charged with the murder, was released from jail and cleared of all charges, according to the State's Attorney's office.

The afternoon papers had barely been on the streets with the story when I got a call in the pressroom from Liam McCafferty.

"Ah, Mr. Malek," he said in his practiced brogue. "I see that your cousin has been cleared."

"Yes, I was planning to call you, but as you can understand, it has been pretty hectic over here."

"Of course, of course, deadlines must be met. Well, sir, I cannot tell you how happy I am to hear the news. Had this tragic event not occurred, I would without question have been able in court to have your cousin found innocent."

"Of that I have no doubt whatsoever, Mr. McCafferty," I said, humoring the attorney.

"As it is, I'm sure you will understand, I have expended a considerable amount of time and effort in preparing Mr. Charles Malek's defense."

"Yes, I understand." I didn't understand, of course, but I was not the least bit interested in prolonging the conversation.

"I thought you would agree with me, sir. Indeed, I knew that you would. Shall I have the bill for my services sent to you?"

"By all means." I gave him my home address.

"You must be very pleased and very happy, Mr. Malek," he said.

"Oh, I am indeed, Mr. McCafferty," I told him, cradling the phone and reveling in the knowledge that my conversations with a lawyer I never met had come to an end.

CHAPTER 22

The next morning at my desk, I reread my piece in the *Trib,* noting that the editors had not changed a single word of my copy. There was no byline, of course, by mutual agreement between me and my bosses. The brass were more than happy to have me write about my own cousin. They just didn't want to broadcast the fact, and for once I totally agreed with a management decision.

I guessed that the gas company wouldn't insist on Charlie returning to work right away, after all that he'd been through. I called him at home and found that I had figured it right.

"Yeah, they said I could take a few days," he said in a tired voice. "Well, I guess it's all over now, isn't it, Stevie?"

"Uh-huh. Hardly a pretty ending though."

"No. Sure isn't."

"How about lunch? Can you come down here around noon? There's a little joint about a block down the street from Headquarters where I usually grab a sandwich." I gave him the address.

"Uh, okay, see you then," he said without enthusiasm.

* * *

Marty's Burger Barn was filled with the usual noisy crowd of cops, lawyers, bondsmen, bailiffs, grifters, and myriad other characters who, by choice or otherwise, found occasion to visit the law enforcement hub of the second-largest city in the land. I had already staked claim to a booth about halfway back along the wall when Charlie pushed in, his eyes scanning the room until he spotted me.

"Quite the busy hangout," he said as he slid in on the opposite side of the table.

"Yeah, you come in here often enough, you'll see everything from assistant state's attorneys to ambulance chasers to pimps to prostitutes to accused axe murderers out on bond. It's a never-ending cavalcade of lawyers and lowlifes–and quite a number of the people in here fall into both those categories."

He nodded, although his thoughts seemed to be far away.

"How are you, Charlie?"

"Okay, I guess," he said listlessly as the waitress came to take our order. We each opted for a burger and coffee.

"She was willing to do anything for you, wasn't she?"

"Huh? Who?"

"Marge, of course."

He knitted his brow. "I guess I don't get you, Stevie."

"Oh, I think you do, Charlie. How long had you

known her?"

Small beads of perspiration began to materialize on his upper lip. "You mean Marge?"

"That's what I said."

"Well, we did grow up near each other."

"That's what I figured, although I don't remember her from the neighborhood, probably because she was so much younger than me–almost a full generation. When I introduced myself to her in Horvath's as your cousin, her first concern seemed to be how you were. She barely mentioned your just-deceased wife, even though they were supposed to be such good pals, at least at the bar. She was what, two or three years younger than you?"

"Something like that."

"Very nice-looking woman."

Charlie nodded vaguely and sipped his coffee. His hand shook.

"As I got to know her, when I was snooping around at Horvath's, it was obvious she wanted me to believe that one of the guys in there did it, probably Johnny Sulski. He's the one who left me this little souvenir," I said, indicating the healing bruise over my eye.

"Geez, I'm sorry about that," he said. "Does it still hurt?"

I told him no, as the burgers were put down in front of us.

"What did you tell her, Charlie?"

He picked up a pickle slice, contemplated it, then set

it back on the plate, pulling in air and letting it out slowly. "We, Marge and me, we started going out just about the time that she graduated from high school. You're right; she was two years younger than me. My mother never liked her, thought she was too wild, too temperamental. You know how my mother could be."

I did indeed. As I had mentioned earlier, Charlie's late mother, my Aunt Edna, was a stern, humorless, controlling sort, and she essentially ran the lives of both her quiet and confrontation-avoiding husband, my now-deceased Uncle Frank, and her only offspring. If she didn't like a friend of Charlie's, she wasn't shy about saying so. Charlie, being something of a milquetoast, wouldn't be likely to defy her, at least openly.

"So, what was the result?"

He shook his head. "We pretty much went out on the sly for a year or so, which was a heckuva way to do things."

"And then...?"

"And then Marge wanted for us to get married."

"How did you feel about that?"

"Stevie, it just wasn't going to happen."

"Go on."

Charlie stared down at his untouched hamburger. "I told Marge I loved her, but that as long as my mother was around..."

"She must have been overjoyed to hear that."

He smiled ruefully. "Yeah, she was on the high-strung side to begin with, and she got really hot. Told me I was a momma's boy, tied to her apron strings. You know that she was right about that, Stevie."

"Then what?"

He took a nibble on his hamburger. I said nothing, waiting him out.

"She started yelling. She told me that we were all through, that she had wasted more than a year on me and wanted to move ahead."

"As in…find somebody else to marry?"

"That's what I figured. And I knew Marge wouldn't have any trouble with that, as attractive and lively as she…was. Within six months, maybe even less, she was engaged to a jerk named Wilson, a pipefitter from somewhere up on the north side–Rogers Park, I think. She ran into him at some dance hall up that way, or so I heard."

"Ever meet him?"

Charlie reddened. "No. I understand what you're saying, Stevie. I shouldn't talk that way about somebody if I didn't even know him. By then, we were in the war, of course, and I got drafted, as you know. I was already overseas in the army when they got married."

"But their marriage didn't last all that long?"

"No, it didn't. Wilson enlisted just a few months after they got married and got killed in the D-Day invasion in June of '44, the very same week that my mother died of cancer. Marge sent me a letter with the news about him and condolences about my mom. She had heard about Mom from one of her relatives in the old neighborhood.

"I was in a military hospital up in the north of England by then, in a part of the country called Yorkshire, almost to Scotland. I think you know I got some leg wounds from shrapnel in the invasion of Italy. God, those were rough times for me. I thought sure I'd be walking with a limp for life, but they fixed me up real good."

"Yes, I knew about all of that from your dad. Nice that you recovered so well. Did Marge say anything else in that letter?"

This time, Charlie took even longer to answer. "Well...she said she'd be waiting for me. The meaning was..."

"Obvious?"

He nodded. "Funny how life is. Now Marge was free and, with my mom gone, so was I. Except that by this time, I had met Edwina. She was volunteering at the hospital where I was laid up, and took a special interest in me, you might say. And do you know, only about three days before I got Marge's letter, I had asked Edwina to marry me."

"I gather that she said yes?"

"She almost jumped into the damn hospital bed with me. I never saw anybody so happy. I thought it was because of me, of course, but eventually I came to figure things out, slow as I am. She wanted a ticket to the U.S., and good old Charlie the Chump Malek was it."

I drank coffee, not wanting to interrupt him now that he was on a roll.

"We got married over there, civil ceremony in the town hall of this little northern English burg, not long after I got out of the hospital. Just a couple of witnesses were present, that was it. I can't even remember the name of the town, although it's probably on the marriage certificate, wherever that is. Everything seemed fine with us until I got discharged a few months later and we came to the States—first me on a troop ship and then Edwina a couple of weeks later on an old passenger liner with a lot of other war brides from all over the place—England, France, Italy, Holland, and so on—hundreds of 'em, so she told me.

"We got settled in the apartment in Pilsen, and almost from the start it seemed like nothing I did was right as far as she was concerned. She didn't like the flat, didn't like the neighborhood, didn't think I had a good enough job, didn't like much of anything. I'm sure you and Catherine saw that pretty quickly when we were all together those few times."

"Hard not to, Charlie."

"Yeah. Then, as you know now, Edwina started going out nights when I was working overtime. Said she felt lonesome and wanted to meet people."

"At Horvath's."

"That's the place. I told her that might not be proper behavior, but she laughed at me and said that in England, the local bars–pubs they're called, as you know–are perfectly respectable places where almost everybody goes to socialize. Or so she said...I never spent much time in the saloons when I was over there, so I don't know if that's really true."

"From what little I saw during my time in London, I'd have to say she was probably right. The few places I visited seemed very friendly."

"Well, anyway, it got so that when I came home from work, usually between nine and ten, Edwina wouldn't even be there most nights. She'd leave me some supper in a pot or two on the stove that I'd have to heat up. Sometimes, she wouldn't get in 'til midnight or even later, sometimes all boozed up and giggly."

"Not a very healthy situation."

"Then one night she comes in, wakes me up, and tells me how she met this really nice gal there–at Horvath's, that is–who knew me."

"Which would, of course, be the newly widowed Marge Blazek."

He took another small bite of his hamburger. "Sure, and they hit it off from the start, so Edwina told me."

"How did they happen to meet?"

"Edwina said that Marge had sat down next to her at the bar and started a conversation."

"Just like that, eh?"

"Yeah, just like that," Charlie agreed. "Some coincidence, wasn't it?"

"If that's what you choose to think, Charlie. But isn't it just possible that Marge knew who Edwina was and who she was married to? Especially since your wife wasn't exactly reticent when it came to talking about herself and her life."

"Well, I guess I never thought about it that way."

"And then you and Marge saw each other again, right?"

He flushed. "It wasn't me that made the first move, Stevie, it was her. About a week after the two of them had met, I'm at home alone–as usual–around ten-thirty at night eating my heated-up supper, and the telephone rings.

"It's Marge, saying that she's calling from the pay phone at Horvath's. I can hear all the noise in the background, the talking and the jukebox. She knows I'm alone, see, because Edwina is sitting at the bar, not thirty feet away from her."

"Yes, I see. From all my recent visits, I know right where that phone is."

"Anyway, Marge says she needs to see me–doesn't say why, but she makes it sound real important."

"Go on."

"So what was I going to do, Stevie?" he asked, his hand shaking again as he picked up his coffee cup and drank.

When I didn't answer, he plunged on.

"So anyway, she says she wants to meet me the next night, at another bar a few blocks west of Horvath's, when

I get off work. A place called Stahlek's. I start to say 'no,' but change my mind before I can get the word out and we agree to meet at this joint the next night at ten." Charlie took a deep breath and looked questioningly at me.

"You're telling the story–go on," I told him.

He sucked in more air, and let it out slowly. "When I got to Stahlek's, it was almost empty. She was sitting at a booth in the corner, the darkest spot in the room, wearing a yellow dress. I'll never forget that yellow dress. She looked terrific, exactly like I remembered her. Not a bit older."

"Cosmetics can work all sorts of magic," I observed dryly.

"Yeah, well, maybe so. But it sure felt funny to see her after all that time. I felt like I was in some sort of a dream."

CHAPTER 23

The lunch crowd in the restaurant had thinned out, but Charlie didn't notice. I signaled the waitress to bring more coffee and take our plates away.

"What did she want to talk about, Charlie?"

"She…sort of beat around the bush at first. Said she just wanted to see me again. Asked me how life was for me now, the job and all."

"And you told her?"

"Well, I started to. I told her that Edwina and I were getting along just fine, and that I was working overtime to save up for a down payment on a house out in the suburbs somewhere.

"But she interrupted me. She said something like 'If you're getting along so well, then why is it that your wife is spending her nights sitting in a bar drinking and flirting with other men?'"

"She was hardly pulling her punches there, was she? How did you respond to that?"

"I tried to laugh it off, but Marge, she saw right through me–she always could, even way back. She told me I was being taken for a ride, and that I *knew* I was being taken for a ride, and that I ought to do something about it."

"Did she have a suggestion?"

"She said I should think real hard about divorcing Edwina. But I told her I couldn't do that because then she would be all alone in a new country without anyone."

"What did Marge say then? Given her reported social activities at Horvath's, it doesn't sound like Edwina would have been all that much alone without you." I was in no mood to spare my cousin's feelings.

Charlie's Adam's apple bobbed up and down as he swallowed hard. "Marge said...well, I'd rather not go into it, Stevie."

I leaned forward, resting both elbows on the table. "Tell you what, cousin. I've always had a lively imagination–both of my wives have told me so. Almost from the beginning of my snooping into this business, I had a suspicion, although I suppressed it, which was my mistake. But this helped confirm that suspicion," I said, pulling some folded sheets from the breast pocket of my suit coat. They were the copy I'd made in Fahey's office of Marge's full suicide note.

"What's that?" Charlie asked.

"I know you've read the newspaper stories about the suicide."

"Yes, I have."

"Well, they mentioned a note that was found at the scene and touched on it briefly."

Charlie nodded, mouth open.

"But there were a lot of details in that note that for reasons I won't go into didn't get into any of the papers, Charlie. Those details plus my own surmising helped me fit the pieces of the puzzle together."

"What puzzle?"

I unfolded the sheets of paper. "Let's see, here we are," I said, smoothing one of the sheets on the tabletop. "Here's what Marge said."

I know I shouldn't have called Charlie, but I couldn't help myself, and when we met, I told him he should get a divorce, but he wouldn't. I could tell that he still loved me, though. That was easy for anybody to see. I told him there might be another way for us. He didn't ask me what I meant, but I think he must have guessed it from his reaction.

His hand jerked in a spasm, jarring his cup and spilling coffee into the saucer. "Now wait a minute, Stevie, that's just not, not–"

"Not what?"

"Not how it happened."

"Okay, how about telling me what did happen."

He ran a hand across his brow. "She–Marge–said that Edwina was the wrong person for me and that we needed to think together about just what could be done."

"Well, that sounds plenty ominous to me."

"But Marge never said anything that night about…about *killing* her."

"Then what did you think she meant at the time, given that you had already ruled out divorce as an option?"

He shrugged. "I guess I really didn't know."

"I think you did know, Charlie, and if I can continue sketching a scenario, you were willing to let Marge take the lead, even steering her in that direction. You said nothing at all to discourage her, right?"

He looked down at the table, silent.

"In fact, if I were to bet, I think you were hopeful that something like what really did happen would occur." I began reading again.

When I went to her flat that night, I knew just what I was going to do. Eddie was surprised to see me there. I'd never been to their place before. I told her I was just passing by, and she invited me in. She showed me around, said the place was a dump, that's the word she used, dump. But it seemed fine to me, just as nice as my apartment, maybe a little nicer.

Then she started talking about Charlie, what a bad provider he was, what a failure he was. It made me so angry, and it made what I was going to do easier. I had brought my own knife just in case, but when she got up to go to the bathroom, I went into the kitchen, got a sharp knife out of a drawer, with a blade maybe five inches long, and slipped it into my purse. This was my original plan—to use one of her own knives. That would make it look like a spur-of-the-moment thing, with the killer attacking her and her grabbing a knife from the kitchen to defend herself.

Eddie came back and wanted to sit on the sofa and talk, so we did. She asked me if I was going to Horvath's later, and I said I was. Then she said she was glad she had that place to hang out in, that it was a lot better than being with Charlie, he was so dull and boring. She called him a shit, said she wished she'd never married him, that it was the biggest mistake of her life, and that she hated him.

That's when I did it. I reached into my purse, took out the knife, and put it in her. She never knew what happened. She didn't say a single word, not one. Just made a kind of sound like a cough and looked up at me, eyes wide, like she was shocked. I was surprised the knife went in so easy and so far, but it did. I wiped off the handle, leaving it still in her, real careful I was, and then I left.

Charlie still looked down at the table, his breath coming in short bursts. I pushed on.

"Marge had planned the visit for around 6:00 o'clock, when you would presumably still be at work on your overtime shift for several more hours," I told him. "That way, she figured you would have an airtight alibi supplied by your gas company co-workers.

"Marge figured a lot of things pretty well, all right, but what she couldn't possibly have known was that this was a rare evening when you weren't working overtime, the reason being that, as you previously told me, construction of a new gas line down in Englewood had to be postponed because the pipe wasn't delivered on time by the manufacturer. You probably came within a few minutes of running into her at your place that night.

"When I told her you hadn't worked overtime that night, she seemed very surprised, which made me suspicious, but again, I suppressed the suspicion. Why would Marge even care what time you got home from work. Unless…"

Charlie looked up at last, tears in his eyes, but he said nothing. I continued:

"When you saw Edwina sprawled on the living room sofa, you had to have known—or strongly suspected—that Marge was the one who drove that knife into her.

"She figured that Sulski or one of the other guys who panted after Edwina in Horvath's would get tagged with the murder and that you and she could dance off into the sunset and live happily ever after.

"On paper, it was a decent enough plan, but it fell apart because you got home at seven or so. Poof went the alibi Marge had so carefully planned for you. She was initially devastated, but she found some hope because I wandered into the picture poking around for suspects. I was the unwitting answer to her prayers. Here's what she said about that."

"No more, Stevie, no more," Charlie said in a shaky voice, holding up his hand and vigorously shaking his head.

"There's plenty more in the note. You need to hear it."

"But, Stevie, I–"

"I insist. Here goes."

When his cousin, this Tribune newspaperman Steve, came into Horvath's doing some investigating-type stuff about Eddie's killing, I got to know him and told him about the guys in the bar who she had liked. I figured that maybe I could get him thinking about one of them as the killer. I felt bad deceiving him, because he seemed like he was a really nice guy, and someone who cared about his cousin.

"I have to say, Charlie, that she really had me going on that. She did indeed deceive me. I would have sworn at that point that one of those four joes had done the killing. She did everything she could to let me know how many men had been chasing after Edwina, and I'm sure she embellished the stories to make your wife sound like a floozy."

"You mean, like even more of a floozy than she really was," Charlie muttered with surprising bitterness.

"If you want to put it that way. I actually thought for a while that another guy, not Sulski, was a prime suspect. Surly fellow named Karl Voyczek, who apparently had spent at least a little time with Edwina outside of Horvath's, as had Ben Barnstable, who was seen walking with her in the neighborhood. But none of that need concern us anymore.

"Moving right along, I was already a little leery on

my last visit to the jail when I asked if you'd had any visitors other than McCafferty, and you hesitated too long before telling me you hadn't. Then Marge's note confirmed that suspicion."

I went and visited Charlie in that terrible jail, and I told him everything. All of it. I said that I had killed Eddie so we could be together at last. I don't think he was the least bit surprised. He seemed to know all along that something like this was going to happen. That's when I told him I was working with his newspaperman cousin to try to get one of Eddie's boyfriends arrested as the murderer.

"That's how it happened, correct?"

Charlie nodded. "She kept saying she wanted for us to get married after this whole thing got cleared up, however that was going to happen. And I told her, right there in the jail, that I was never going to marry her. Never."

"Yep. That squares with the note. To continue:"

That's when he told me he could never love me anymore, not after what I did. I just gave up then. My life was at a dead end.

"Sounds pretty melodramatic, Charlie."

"She started bawling right there in the jail, telling me that I was the only one she had ever loved. Ever. She got sort of hysterical. A guard finally came over and asked her to leave."

"And knowing how tightly strung she was normally, you probably weren't shocked when you learned that she killed herself."

Tears formed in his eyes. "No, Stevie, I was shocked. Really I was, and very, very sad. That's the truth, Stevie, the truth."

"But you were not sad to learn that she had confessed," I said. Charlie looked away.

"Something I'm curious about before we finish this," I said, forcing him to meet my glare. "You couldn't have known that Marge was going to visit you in the Bridewell. What if she had never shown up?"

He raised his shoulders slightly and let them drop. "I guess that...what I thought was going to happen all along was that there'd be a trial, and that I'd be..." He let it hang.

"Well, that's one point in your favor, Charlie, although a small one. At least you were willing to take the fall for what was partly your doing anyway." I turned to the final page of the note. "There's just a little left," I told him.

"No more, please," he whined. "No more, Stevie."

"You need to hear it all," I spat. "Everything that was kept out of the papers–by me, goddammit! I want you to hear every word. "

I'm a sinner in so many ways, and what I'm going to do now, I know, is also a sin in the eyes of the church. But it's what I deserve. I have an aching soul. To my dear cousin Gladys and your fine husband Herb, please give my love to your beautiful little girls, Mandie and Patsy. Tell them their Aunty Marge is going away on a long trip, but that she will always think of them and love them wherever she is.

"It's as if you put that knife in Edwina yourself," I said, bearing down on each word as if I were typing them in a frenzy. "And then pushed Marge into that train. You might as well have. You knew how unbalanced she was, probably even more so since her husband's death. You knew she wanted you back, even though you didn't want her yourself anymore. You probably even suspected she might kill herself after what you told her on her trip to the jail. What you didn't know was that she would leave a note behind that got you off the hook—or rather, out of the electric chair. Must have been a wonderful surprise for you. Even in death, she gave you more than you deserved."

"What are you going to do, Stevie?" my cousin asked. He had never seemed more pathetic to me than at that moment.

I shook my head and stood. "Not a damn thing, Charlie. Not one single damn, blessed thing. You've lost the two women closest to you in the world—after your mother, that is. That's enough punishment for a lifetime, as far as I'm concerned." I dropped a tip on the table and went to the front counter to pay the bill. I couldn't stand to look at him any more.

"I'll split it with you," Charlie said, following after me.

"Nope, this one's on me all the way," I replied,

unsmiling.

As we stepped out onto the sidewalk, Charlie held out a hand. "Well, Stevie...I guess I'll be seeing you," he said, giving me a tentative smile.

"No, Charlie, I don't believe that you will," I told him, ignoring the outstretched paw. I turned away and headed back south on State Street to Police Headquarters.

CHAPTER 24

Fergus Fahey and I never spoke about Edwina or Marge or Charlie, not a single word. I didn't want to bring the subject up, and I'm sure he didn't, either. I wondered if he ever hauled Charlie in for questioning after the suicide, but I figured he–and the department–were happy to close the case with Marge's death and written confession.

After all, what could they have charged Charlie with, anyway? He really hadn't done anything but possibly encourage Marge's actions by his rejection of her. If that were a crime, new prisons would have to be constructed every month.

I never saw my cousin again. I did forward Liam McCafferty's hefty bill to him, though, and can only assume that he paid it, since I never heard from the celebrated lawyer. Charlie sent us Christmas cards for a couple of years, but then stopped, probably because we didn't reciprocate.

I learned from another cousin that he had gotten married and was living in a bungalow in some western suburb, Brookfield I think it was, or maybe North Riverside. And then I heard later that he'd gotten divorced and had moved into an apartment in that area. To lift a line from the end of a book by Scott Fitzgerald that I read once, "in any case, he is almost certainly in that section of the country, in one town or another."

Peter got his summer internship at Frank Lloyd Wright's Taliesin up in the Wisconsin countryside. The architect had held true to his promise to make an exception for him after my long interview with him ran in the Sunday *Tribune*–with color photographs of Wright at work, as well as shots of his Fallingwater house in Pennsylvania and his Johnson's Wax headquarters in Racine, Wis. I even got a handwritten letter from the man himself, acknowledging that my article, which was by no means fawning, "was pretty much on the mark, at least as far as it went."

He did take issue with one line in the story, however, in which I wrote that Wright "was in the very front rank of American architects, along with Ludwig Mies van der Rohe, Edward Durrell Stone, and Eero Saarinen."

"I AM the front rank of American architects, period!" Wright fired back the very next day, adding that "None of them is even fit to carry my t-square."

Peter said the Taliesin experience overall was a good one, even though he spent much of his time doing such menial chores as slopping hogs and building a henhouse as part of the regimen at that unorthodox communal enclave, where everybody was expected to get their hands dirty.

In the asset column, Wright wrote in the same letter that "Your lad acquitted himself well here and was a hard worker. We can only hope that on his return to that cow college mired in the Illinois cornfields, he will resist the pedestrian design suggestions and theories of his instructors." Wright himself had critiqued Peter's drafting exercises and even complimented him on preliminary sketches he had done of a proposed single-family home, a home that Peter says he plans to build one day for himself and the wife he has yet to meet.

Also on the plus side, the experience earned him some stature when he returned to the architecture school at the University of Illinois the following fall. This despite the fact that some of the professors viewed Wright as unorthodox, eccentric, and even a "charlatan," as one faculty member termed him.

But Peter said that, to a man, his instructors were impressed that he had gotten an inside look at the workings of this singular fellowship and the self-proclaimed "greatest architect in the world" who presided over his pastoral realm like a feudal lord.

The End

EPILOGUE

The preceding is entirely a work of fiction, and any instances in which historical figures interact with fictional ones are solely the products of the author's imagination. The people and events discussed below were researched by the author in regard to specific dates and occurrences. In addition, some of Frank Lloyd Wright's quotes were taken from biographies. The comment by Wright about fellow architect Eero Saarinen was recounted by the author's father, himself an architect, who attended a talk Wright had given. A bibliography of volumes read as part of that research follows this epilogue.

Frank Lloyd Wright (1867-1959) was without question the best-known architect of his era, a period that spanned an amazing seven decades. Early on, in Chicago, his work was influenced by his mentor, the great Louis Sullivan. By the early years of the Twentieth Century, while still in his thirties, Wright made a national name for himself with his revolutionary "Prairie Style" houses, which sprang up in his hometown of Oak Park, Ill., as well as in numerous other Chicago suburbs, and then spread throughout the country.

In the ensuing decades, the flamboyant and controversial Wright saw his career undergo numerous peaks and valleys. His greatest works include Tokyo's Imperial Hotel, which withstood a tumultuous earthquake in the 1920s; his daring 1937 masterpiece, "Fallingwater," cantilevered over a waterfall in Pennsylvania; the Johnson's Wax headquarters complex in Racine, Wis.; and New York's Guggenheim Museum. The Guggenheim, his only New York City building, was completed after his death in 1959, just short of his ninety-second birthday.

Unity Temple, in Oak Park, Ill., is an iconic Frank Lloyd Wright work. Constructed from 1905 to 1908, it is a historic landmark and has been honored by the American Institute of Architects for its design. Built for a Universalist congregation, the temple now serves as a Unitarian-Universalist place of worship, the two denominations having merged in 1961.

World War II War Brides. Following the end of the Second World War in 1945, U.S. servicemen by the thousands brought home brides from Europe and Asia. Although specific figures are hard to come by, it has been estimated that more than 100,000 American soldiers, sailors, marines, and airmen married women from the United Kingdom alone during and immediately following the war. Thousands of other GIs married and brought to this country women from France, the Netherlands,

Belgium, Italy, Germany, Australia, the Philippines, Japan, and other nations that had an American military presence during the war.

The Naperville, Ill. train wreck. On April 25, 1946, a Burlington Route streamlined passenger limited, the California-bound Exposition Flyer, crashed at high speed into another passenger train, the Advance Flyer, which was stopped in Naperville, a suburb some 30 miles west of Chicago. A total of 39 passengers and six Burlington employees were killed, and another 110 persons were injured, making it one of the deadliest railroad mishaps in U.S. history.

The Suzanne Degnan murder investigation was brought to a conclusion in August 1946 with the arrest of 17-year-old University of Chicago student William Heirens. After intense and likely brutal interrogation and an injection of truth serum, Heirens confessed to the murders of the six-year-old Degnan girl and two Chicago women, Josephine Ross in June 1945 and Frances Brown in December. It was in the Brown apartment after her murder that the killer wrote in lipstick on a mirror: "For heaven's sake, catch me before I kill more. I cannot control myself." This resulted in the newspapers referring to the murderer as "the Lipstick Killer."

The confession was part of a plea bargain that guaranteed him immunity from execution. Heirens, who has steadfastly maintained his innocence and has numerous supporters, said that "I confessed to live." A prisoner for 60 years as of this writing, the 77-year old Heirens is an inmate at the Dixon Correctional Center in Illinois.

BIBLIOGRAPHY

As in the previous Snap Malek mysteries, microfilm of old newspapers was invaluable as a research tool. In this book, information about the era was gleaned specifically from microfilm files of the *Chicago Tribune* from the early months of 1946, the first postwar year. Following are other sources that were used:

Cannon, Patrick. *Hometown Architect: The Complete Buildings of Frank Lloyd Wright in Oak Park and River Forest, Ill.* San Francisco: Pomegranate Communications, 2006.

Friedland, Roger and Zellman, Harold. *The Fellowship: The Untold Story of Frank Lloyd Wright & the Taliesin Fellowship.* New York: Regan, 2006.

Kisor, Henry. *Zephyr: Tracking a Dream Across America.* New York: Times Books, 1994. (Helpful for details of the Naperville, Ill., Chicago, Burlington & Quincy Railroad train collision of 1946.)

McCullough, David. *Truman.* New York: Simon &

Schuster, 1992. (Helpful for information about the labor turmoils in the U.S. in the immediate postwar period.)

Shukert, Elfrieda Berthiaume and Scibetta, Barbara Smith. *War Brides of World War II.* San Francisco: Presidio Press, 1988.

Wendt, Lloyd. *Chicago Tribune: The Rise of a Great American Newspaper.* Chicago: Rand-McNally & Co., 1979.

Coming

Fall 2008

TO KILL A PRESIDENT

A Snap Malek Mystery

Book Four

Turn the page to read an excerpt...

Chapter 1

October 1948

"Truman's gonna get murdered next month, absolutely murdered," Dirk O'Farrell of the *Chicago Sun Times* pronounced as he leaned back with his feet on the desk and blew smoke rings toward the grimy, flaking ceiling of the Police Headquarters press room. "I still stick with what I been saying since summer: the Democrats were nuts to nominate the guy, even if he is the incumbent."

"Afraid I can't agree there, Dirk," rumbled Anson Masters of the *Daily News*. "The working men, the union men, will all rally to him, and their wives will vote the way they do. Always have, always will."

"Oh, hell, Antsy, you can't be serious," O'Farrell shot back, jabbing his cigarette toward Masters as if it were a midget's fencing sword. "Harry's losing big chunks of Democrats all over the place. You've got them Dixiecrats from down south, as they like to call themselves, who jumped the party and have that Strom Thurmond character from South Carolina running. He'll take votes away from Truman all across the damn South. And then there's that pinko Henry Wallace and his wacky

Progressives, they'll eat into his support even more, especially in places like New York. Dewey'll romp home. Take it to the bank."

"What's *your* take, Snap?" asked Packy Farmer of Hearst's *Herald-American,* snapping his suspenders. "The way your *Tribune* is beating the drum for Dewey and hammering away at Harry—no surprise there—one would think by reading its pages that the election's just a formality."

I set the three-star edition of the *Trib* down on the desk and took a long drag on my Lucky Strike. "May surprise you boys to learn that I agree with my esteemed *Daily News* colleague," I said, gesturing toward Masters. "Fact is, I believe that Anson's got it right, although this may sound strange, coming from one who takes his checks from the dear old *Tribune*."

"Indeed!" Farmer guffawed. "And I won't quote you, Snap. I understand that Colonel McCormick fires anyone who doesn't hew to the ol' party line. But honestly, why do you think Truman's got a chance?"

"First off, Packy, let me clear one thing up. The Colonel may be a rock-ribbed Republican, but he's got a healthy share of Democrats scattered around in his newsroom, and I suspect he knows it—and grudgingly lives with it. As to the election: Like he proved when he ran against FDR in '44, Dewey's a stiff. Pompous is too generous a word for him. He works crowds with all the warmth and grace of the maitre d' at the snootiest restaurant in town. And he even looks like a maitre d' for God's sake, with that cute little mustache of his. The guy just doesn't connect with the average joe. And this country's filled with average joes. My paper may have already put Tom Dewey in the White House, but I'm not buying it."

The above badinage is typical of our mornings in the pressroom at Police Headquarters, 1121 S. State St., Chicago USA. At this point, I should set the stage.

The cast of characters–and I'd have to say we qualify as characters, present company included–all have been long-time police reporters on the city's four big daily papers. Anson Masters of the *Daily News* has been around longer than the rest of us, a fact that he is not shy about mentioning at every opportunity. The long-divorced Masters, with a bald, freckled and ruddy pate, must be pushing seventy now, but if he has any plans to hang it up and go fishing someplace, I've never heard them. My guess is he'll be carried out of the pressroom in that proverbial pine box.

The *Herald-American's* Packy Farmer, also divorced, is about the same age as Masters, but he wears his years somewhat better. Even with his once-black hair yielding to gray, he still has the look of a riverboat gambler with his center part and thin mustache. And to further the image, he plays a mean game of five-card stud, as I've learned to my regret.

The lanky, white-haired Dirk O'Farrell, who toils for the newly formed *Sun-Times*, had previously been with Hearst's old *Herald and Examiner* and then with the *Sun,* a forerunner paper to his current employer. When the *Sun* and the *Times* merged in February of '48, Dirk got the pressroom job, squeezing out Eddie Metz, who had been the *Times* man at Police Headquarters for years. That was a good call, as O'Farrell is twice the newsman as Metz, which isn't saying a lot. Last I heard, Eddie, who should be in another line of work–maybe slinging burgers in a hash house–was employed in the *Sun-Times* morgue, where he can't do a lot of damage.

That leaves me, Steve "Snap" Malek, age forty-four. I got the moniker because I wear snap-brim hats, sometimes indoors as well as out, although my late and sainted mother would have been appalled at that breach of etiquette. I've been with the *Tribune* for almost all of my professional life, the last fifteen years of it on this beat except for a short stint in England as a foreign correspondent in the closing year of World War II. And if you'll allow me to dispense with the false modesty, I'm by far the best writer of the bunch in this pressroom, and the best reporter as well.

So why am I hanging around this dreary room in this dreary building, you ask? Because I'm basically lazy. I've had other opportunities at the paper, including general assignment reporting, where I would have roved all over the city, covering everything from gangland killings to hotel fires to ward elections to airplane crashes and train wrecks. But I've turned down these opportunities, in part because I like the day shift.

Years ago, I preferred working days because it left my evenings open for drinking, something I used to do far too often, destroying a marriage and almost a career in the process. Now I still prefer working days, but for a different reason: I'm happily remarried and commute home every night on the Lake Street Elevated Line to Catherine and our stucco house on a shady street in the quiet near-western suburb of Oak Park.

Actually, it's *her* stucco house, the one she grew up in and has lived in most of her life, except for the few unhappy years of her own first marriage. I would have preferred living in the city, but Catherine loves the house and the village, where she works as an assistant librarian at the public library.

We have no children of our own, although I've got a son, Peter, from my marriage to Norma. He's in his final year of the architecture program at the University of Illinois in Champaign. Two summers ago, he had the singular experience of toiling up at Taliesin in Wisconsin for Frank Lloyd Wright, the self-professed greatest architect in the world. Peter claims that stint will help guarantee him a job with a Chicago firm after graduation. I hope he's right.

So there in capsule form are my private and professional lives–other than to mention that I have a tendency, as a reporter, to pursue some stories more aggressively than both my wife and the police would prefer. On one occasion, I came close to catching a fatal bullet, on a second I would have been strangled but for an alert college student, and on a third, I found myself trading punches on a Southwest Side street with a burly construction worker while several of his bar habitués looked on–hardly a neutral audience.

For the last dozen or so years, my job at Police Headquarters has been to cover the Detective Bureau, which is the most wide-ranging beat in the building. I was nominated for this by my fellow reporters, who pointed out that the biggest job at Headquarters should go to the guy at the biggest paper, and which also has the biggest news hole to fill.

But that's only part of the story. Because we all share our news with one another, making a mockery of the term "competitive journalism," everything each of us gets from our respective beats goes to all the others so that nobody gets "scooped" and gets chewed out by their city editor. And although I've already conceded my laziness, I am in fact the least lazy of this pressroom foursome. So I usually get the juiciest news in the building–and immediately have to share it.

So on this morning like all others, I trundled down one flight to the office of Fergus Sean Fahey, Chicago's longtime chief of detectives. I was greeted in the small anteroom by Fahey's secretary, Elsie Dugo Cascio. "Nice to see you, intrepid reporter," she said, looking up from the typewriter with her ever-present toothy smile.

"The feeling is mutual," I replied with a bow. "Is himself on the premises this fine morning?"

"He is indeed." She announced me over the intercom and got a squawk that sounded vaguely like "Send him in."

"Nice to see you, Fergus," I said, tossing a half-full pack of Lucky Strikes on his blotter.

"I'd rather be fishing," he muttered, looking up from a stack of paperwork and pulling a cigarette out of the pack. "I s'pose you want coffee?"

"Good guess," I said as he reached for the intercom to signal Elsie. But she was already coming through the doorway with a steaming cup of java.

"You pamper me," I told her with a grin. "Don't ever stop."

"You say the sweetest things to a girl," she purred, turning on her heel and leaving, closing the door behind her.

"One in a million," I observed. "The other gal you had here taking her place seemed okay, and she made decent-enough coffee. But you've got to be glad to have Elsie back again."

"Yeah, I am, but call me a traditionalist, Snap. A mother really ought to be home with her little one," Fahey said with a sigh. "Her sister over on Ashland Boulevard is watching the little guy during the day now."

"Is the money tight at home?"

Fahey took a drag on his Lucky and shrugged. "Seems that her husband does okay working in the purchasing department at that railroad, the Rock Island Line. But they're saving up to buy a house in the suburbs. There's a neighborhood they like out in Elmhurst, I think it is. They need Elsie's extra income for a down payment, so I figure she'll be here another year or so."

"At least the kid's in good hands with an aunt," I said. "It's not like Elsie's leaving him with some stranger."

"True enough," the chief replied without enthusiasm. "How's things on the home front for you?"

"No complaints. Catherine's still working at the Oak Park Library, which she loves. And Peter's going to graduate down in Champaign in the spring. Still lives with his mother and her husband over on Lake Shore Drive, but I figure he'll get himself a place in the city after graduation–as well as a job with an architectural firm. Enough on family life. What's percolating in your department, Fergus?"

He snorted. "Big worry all over the department right now is Truman's visit to town next week. Never fun when a President comes around."

"Hmm? You expecting trouble?"

Fahey ground out his cigarette. "Presidents make me nervous. There's a lot of nut cases out there. Remember FDR down in Miami back in '33?"

"Lot of folks think Cermak really was the target, not

Roosevelt," I said, referring to Chicago Mayor Anton Cermak, who was shot dead by an assassin while sitting on a dais next to the President-elect.

"Maybe. I'd still rather that Harry stayed out of town."

"Well, Fergus, it's the home stretch of a tough campaign, and our President is not about to pass up a chance to show his smiling mug in the second-largest city of this great land. There's votes to be had, and 'Give 'em Hell Harry' wants–and needs–those votes."

"Shit, he figures to win Illinois anyway," Fahey said, torching another Lucky. "Why not have him stump in some of the states where he's running behind in the polls?"

"Beats me, Fergus. But I still think you're worrying over nothing. Nobody's going to take a potshot at him. Not with all the security both the Feds and your own force are going to be providing."

"I suppose you're right," the chief of detectives answered, but his voice seemed to lack conviction.

THREE STRIKES YOU'RE DEAD
A Snap Malek Mystery

Book One

SHADOW OF THE BOMB
A Snap Malek Mystery

Book Two

Robert Goldsborough
Interviews
Max Allan Collins

If Max Allan Collins is not the most productive writer in the mystery and suspense field, I would be hard-pressed to find another nominee. He has written more than eighty novels, many of them components of seven different series. His works include his fourteen highly acclaimed Nate Heller books, the CSI series, and the *New York Times* bestseller "Saving Private Ryan."

In addition, he has been a scripter of the "Dick Tracy" comic strip, and his graphic novel "Road to Perdition" was the source of the film starring Tom Hanks, Paul Newman, and Stanley Tucci. He also is a screenwriter and independent filmmaker. He has won the Private Eye Writers of America Shamus Award (twice) and the Bouchercon Anthony Award, and has been nominated for the Mystery Writers of America's Edgar Award in both fiction and non-fiction categories.

Max has long been an inspiration to me, among other reasons because of his ability to brilliantly blend real and fictional characters in his novels, many set against the backdrop of actual events, including the Lindbergh kidnapping, Amelia Earhart's doomed final flight, and Huey Long's assassination.

I recently asked Max to share some of his thoughts about

mixing fact and fiction in mystery/suspense writing. Following is our conversation.

–Robert Goldsborough

Goldsborough: In so many of your novels, you have mixed historical figures with your fictional ones. Are there historical figures–or types–who are especially attractive to you as subjects?

Collins: I'm particularly interested in exploring figures in 20th century history who have fed the popular culture– Eliot Ness, Al Capone, Wyatt Earp. To me, it's fascinating to see the reality behind the myth. I'm not myth-busting, though. The three I mentioned led lives fully worthy of generating myths. And always the truth about such figures is more interesting than the Hollywood versions.

Along those same lines, I've tried to examine the private eye myth in its historical context. The hardboiled/noir private eye became a part of the popular culture when Hammett and Chandler defined the character as a genre hero in the '20s, '30s, and '40s. I wanted to dig into the convention and even the clichés of the P.I. in a historical context. Usually in the Nate Heller novels, Heller stands in for the real investigator, often a private eye or insurance investigator. That way, he doesn't feel shoehorned in.

Goldsborough: In several books, you have used famous events as your centerpiece. Do you go to the places where these events occurred? And if you do, do you find the visit gives you a better understanding of the historical event(s)?

Collins: With my primary research associate, George Hagenauer, I've visited virtually all of the Chicago locations in the Nate Heller memoirs. We did a big walking tour of the Loop in '81, and much of what we saw then is gone now. Sometimes time or money makes it impossible for me to visit a location, so I turn to others. I had a friend who was teaching on Saipan take photos and do research there for "Flying Blind," the Amelia Earhart novel. But I did to go Nassau for "Carnal Hours" and to Hawaii for "Damned in Paradise." Seeing the actual place is helpful–it's like location scouting for a film. It's not until you see how tiny the pillars are at the Baton Rouge Capitol–which Long's assassin supposedly hid behind, lying in wait, a physical impossibility–that certain questions start popping into your brain.

Goldsborough: Any anecdotes about those visits?

Collins: Probably the most memorable was sitting around the pool at the Flamingo in Vegas with a retired pit boss who had worked the opening weekend of the casino/hotel. He dispelled the story that the opening was a flop–it wasn't, it was huge–but Ben "Bugsy" Siegel hadn't finished enough hotel rooms, meaning his customers stayed at other hotels and did much of their gambling off-site. He also pointed out several rose bushes under which he claimed certain disloyal employees had gone to rest.

Another prime anecdote had to do with a Cleveland trip George Hagenauer made without me. We did numerous Cleveland visits researching Eliot Ness. George was checking out Kingsbury Run, the nasty gully where the Mad Butcher did his thing, and got chased by a pack of wild dogs for his trouble.

Goldsborough: As a result of writing about real people, have you ever gotten any reaction from their descendants?

Collins: I've had very positive contact with friends and relatives of Sally Rand and Barney Ross, both recurring characters in the Heller novels. Film director William Friedkin, who liked "True Detective," was a nephew or something of one of the crooked cops in that book. The most trouble I've had came from Amelia Earhart fans who were furious that I depicted her as bisexual. I do the research and calls 'em as I sees 'em.

Goldsborough: Do you have any general advice for mystery writers who want to mix fact and fiction in their work?

Collins: The biggest temptation is to put in every scrap of research. You remember the long hours you put in, plus you get fascinated with the subject in a way that doesn't always jibe with the novelist's mission to entertain. The research that shows in the book is the tip of the iceberg that (a) allows the reader to extrapolate the rest of the iceberg, and (b) provides solid if off-stage underpinning that makes the writer confident that the time and place are being shared with the reader.

MEET THE AUTHOR

In his early teens, Robert Goldsborough complained to his mother one summer day that he had "nothing to do." An avid reader of Rex Stout's Nero Wolfe mysteries, she gave him a magazine serialization, and he became hooked on the adventures of the corpulent Nero and his irreverent sidekick, Archie Goodwin.

Through his school years and beyond, Goldsborough devoured virtually all of the 70-plus Wolfe mysteries. It was during his tenure as writer and editor with the *Chicago Tribune* that the paper printed the obituary of Rex Stout. On reading it, his mother lamented that "Now there won't be any more Nero Wolfe stories."

"There might be *one* more," Goldsborough mused, and began writing an original Wolfe novel for his mother as a 1978 Christmas present. This story, *Murder in E Minor*, remained a bound typescript for years, but in the mid-'80s, Goldsborough received permission from the Stout estate to publish it. *Murder in E Minor* first appeared as a Bantam hardcover, then in paperback, and six more Nero Wolfe novels eventually followed–all to favorable reviews.

As much as he enjoyed writing those mysteries, Robert Goldsborough longed to create his own characters. Thus, so far we have *Three Strikes You're Dead*, set in the gang-ridden Chicago of the late 1930s; *Shadow of the Bomb*, set in the early years of America's participation in World War II as scientists worked to secretly develop the atomic bomb on the University of Chicago campus, and *A Death in Pilsen*, set during the postwar mid-1940s in an old southside Chicago neighborhood–each book in the series narrated by *Tribune* police reporter Steve Malek.

Goldsborough, a lifelong Chicagoan who logged twenty-one years with the *Tribune* and twenty-three years with the trade journal *Advertising Age*, says it was "Probably inevitable that I would end up using a newspaperman as my protagonist."